DRAGON'S DESTINY

RED PLANET DRAGONS OF TAJSS BOOK TWENTY

MIRANDA MARTIN

CONTENTS

I've been searching for my mate. For my destiny. For the female who is somewhere on Tajss...

Khabri

The Zmaj race was dying when humans crashed landed on our planet. Since the moment their coming was revealed to the Order, I've known that one of the females is my mate. My treasure. All I want is her and the beautiful, perfect babies we will have together.

When at long last I find her, there can be no mistaking our connection. My dragon roars with possessive need and the claim is made.

Except she has other ideas. She doesn't believe in destiny and says she isn't interested in making babies with me.

The Invaders are threatening all of Tajss, thrusting her peoples into war. I must survive these battles if I am to have a chance at winning the one that matters. The war for Anna's heart.

Anna

My village has been overrun by four-armed invaders and we've all been forced to flee towards the city.

We're struggling to survive pursuit over the grueling desert sands of Tajss when a crazy, overly muscled, overly sexy, and overly direct alien dragon-man shows up and tells me I'm his fated mate and we're going to make beautiful babies.

I don't think so.

Except he *is* sexy. And kind. And protective. And he might be the only hope I have of living. Can I put my past beliefs behind me, navigate a war and deal with losing my heart all at the same time?

Celebrate the 20th book in the Red Planet Dragons of Tajss series! The couple's story in Dragon's Destiny is stand-alone with an HEA, but the story of planet Tajss is told over the entire series. It is a science fiction romance with a stub-

born alien and an equally stubborn human female, plenty of action-packed adventure, and hot, steamy alien romance!

1

KHABRI

I STALK THE CITY, SEARCHING. SHE'S HERE. SHE MUST BE. THE one. My one. This longing won't stop until I find her. Until she is mine. Filled with my seed, bearing my children.

Long dark hair ripples and shines in the corner of my vision. I look towards it so fast my neck cracks. No. It is a female, but it is not her.

It has been years since we were ordered to look for the humans. The Eye had predicted their crashing to Tajss and gave us our orders. I knew, the moment the prediction was read to the Council. My dragon roared to life, right there in the Council chambers, staking my claim as if she were there with us.

Could it be wrong? Am I mistaking this feeling? Is it something else?

Archion stops and points at the fountain. The ancient statue of Estrogan declaring victory. Once I admired Estrogan, the hero of my childhood, but now I know he was a fool. It was a false victory, an empty freedom he declared. A war waged for nothing.

Before the Devastation, the fountain spouted water into the air three wingspans high and created sparkling rainbows as it tinkled down to the pool at the base. Now the water barely trickles, but the pool is about half full and many humans gather around it.

"They've gotten the water running, and it's pure. They use it for drinking, cooking, and cleaning," Archion says with pride, as if he himself performed this small miracle.

"I see," I say, purposely keeping my voice cool.

His enthusiasm is undampened. He leads me through the City, pointing out with great self-importance the improvements the humans and Zmaj living here have accomplished. It is impressive, but the longing in my guts and the ache in my cock distract me.

Where is she? Have I been wrong? All the females living with the Tribe are mated, so she cannot be there. She must be here.

"Councilor," Archion says, cutting through my thoughts.

"Do NOT call me that here," I growl. Archion's mouth snaps shut. He stands at attention before nodding his head. Nearby humans stop what they are doing to stare. "Or do that."

"Yes Counc--," he stops himself. "Khabri."

My name emerges through gritted teeth. He shakes his head and the conflict on his face is plain to see. It goes against all his training not to refer to me by my title, but he should know better. He's been drilled on the need for secrecy. It is part of his Oaths! When we return to the compound, I will have him punished. No matter our friendly relations with the humans, I am under orders of my own, even as he is. They are not to know my rank. The Order reveals only what we wish, what we are told.

Except the Order is without orders. We lost contact with the Southern Continent and haven't been able to reestablish it. We've been left blind and directionless. Archion has no idea. He's a Scout and that knowledge is not for him.

Councilor Tashak is Seer in title only. The true sight was not gifted to him. Only The Eye has that gift, and we have lacked his guidance. We've been left to operate on our own and do the best we are able, furthering the broader goals of Tajss itself.

Our last orders were not to engage the humans, to watch them, help without being found out, and wait. Archion and his brother Khal destroyed those orders, but it doesn't mean we've opened our doors in full to the humans. Keeping them on the outside is best until we know more. Until we reestablish contact with The Eye. Only then can we know the will of Tajss with certainty.

Except for the one thing I do know.

My mate is here. Impossible as it is, she exists. This fire, this gnawing, aching emptiness won't be denied. The instant the Council received the message to find the humans, my dragon raged to life, staking a claim sight unseen, knowing in its own way that my match is among them.

Archion resumes the tour he is giving me of the City and their work. I don't tell him it's not my first journey here or that I am already familiar with everything he points to with pride. Pride as if he himself accomplished all these works, whereas I know he did nothing of the sort.

The industriousness of the human race is apparent. They have transformed Draconov from an empty ruin haunted by a lone Zmaj to something at least habitable. It is nothing compared to the City in its glory, prior to the Devastation of course, but that does not lessen their accomplishments.

I listen with half an ear, studying every group of humans we encounter. Hoping that this time will be the one, that I will find her. My mate. The female who will bear my children, whom my soul yearns for, the one Tajss intends to be mine.

It hurts, physically. My stomach cramps, my cock randomly stiffens and aches, and there is a building pressure in my head. I'm quick to anger and distracted.

"Cou-Khabri," Archion says. "Do you not approve?"

I glare, not letting his slip pass unnoticed. Purposely, I frown and narrow my eyes while stilling my tail, expressing my displeasure. The coloration of his scales shifts to softer, dimmer colors, acknowledging my upset.

"Have I said otherwise?" I ask, though I have no idea why he is asking me if I approve or what he is referring to with his question.

"No, Khabri," he says.

"When I do not approve, you will know it," I snap. "I wish to see more of the humans working."

I want to find her, I think but do not say aloud.

"Of course," Archion says, leading the way through the City streets.

We survey their work while none of the humans pay us any particular attention. The suns are low in the sky when we've finished our tour. My head is pounding and the horns on my head throb with each beat of my hearts. Nothing. Still. She's here, she must be, this feeling can't be wrong, can it?

"Have we seen all the humans?" I ask as we walk alone to the airlock.

Archion frowns as his eyes dart towards me but he keeps facing ahead. It's an odd question and he obviously has questions he doesn't speak. He scratches his neck then shakes his head.

"I would say no," he says. "I don't know the exact population, but we saw the majority if not all of it."

"Do we not have an accounting of them?" I ask.

"No sir," he answers.

"Why not?" I ask.

"Sir, one was never ordered," he says, staring ahead as we continue walking.

The buildings closest to the dome are in the worst condition.

4

The humans and their Zmaj mates have stayed close to the center of the City, congregating apart but not too far apart. The original damage to the City is clearly written here.

I remember Draconov in its glory. As a member of the Order Council I was trained in methods of holding the bijass at bay. Keeping history is part of my duty. I was not granted the luxury of forgetting the horrors of our past. Well do I know the horror of war.

"None of the humans contracted the illness?" I ask.

"No sir," he says. "It affected the Zmaj only, but Addison believes that the humans were carrying the virus."

I nod understanding. This agrees with our research, adding veracity to the medical findings.

"Is anyone still ill?" I ask.

"No sir," he says. "Rosalind and Visidion ordered the City into a lock-down, limiting exposure. They were able to stop the virus, and Addison came up with a cure if anyone does become ill again."

Archion doesn't ask questions about the reason for my visit, but I know he has them. All of the information he's shown me has already been reported to the Council, but reading dry reports is not the same as direct questioning, I have always found. We are in sight of the airlock which we exit in silence. The human on guard duty will not be privy to my private conversations.

Once we're outside and alone again, I let the silence extend. The warmth of the setting suns soaks into my scales, bringing some semblance of relief from the empty ache. Thankfully, the pain in my head recedes too.

"How are they doing militarily?" I ask.

"Sir?" he asks, actually looking at me with a quizzical expression.

"Militarily," I repeat.

"They aren't, sir," he says.

"Yet they've fought off the Invaders," I observe.

"Yes sir," he agrees.

"And Ladon found his way to that military base," I say.

"Yes sir," he says.

"So I pose the question again," I say. "How are they doing militarily?"

He doesn't answer for several strides. I let him organize his thoughts. We have a long journey back to the compound. I study him as we walk and suddenly a fire ignites in my chest. My hearts burn, my limbs grow heavy, and my stomach clenches. How is it he has found his mate and I haven't? An urge to strike him surges and I ball my hands into fists but manage to stop myself before I act.

"They are weak, but determined," he says. "The humans are tenacious. They possess an inner strength that is highly admirable."

"Even the females?"

"Especially the females," he answers.

"I see," I say.

We travel back to the compound in silence. Archion looks askance in my direction a few times, but I let him stew. I'm lost in my own thoughts and do not have time for his concerns. We drop into one of the hidden tunnels and before long we're emerging past the posted guards who snap to attention as I walk past.

"Archion, report for punishment for breach of secrecy protocols," I say without bothering to look at him.

I feel him bristle as his bijass rises in response, but he doesn't act on it. Instead he snaps to attention.

"Yes sir," he says.

I stride through the compound, taking the halls that will be least traveled. I'll make my report to the Council in the morning. Tonight I want to be alone.

Behind my closed doors I slip off the plain loose robe I wore to blend in at the City. My prime cock is stiff and throbs painfully, but I ignore it. Naked I go to my water bowl which is kept full by my assistant. I rinse my eyes then place cool water on my cock, trying to calm my raging desire for a female that I haven't seen.

My cock jumps, my stomach clenches, and my balls tighten. I close my eyes to focus, to think of nothing. I empty my mind of thought and emotion. Or I try.

I can't.

In the blackness behind my eyelids is swirling desire. A storm assaulting my control. I breathe in, then exhale slowly, repeating this cycle over and over, but it doesn't help.

An impression of her consumes my attention. She's perfect in every way. Fine, strong hips perfect for the bearing of many children. This is the future that was predicted so long ago. That we would emerge from the Devastation, not unharmed, but stronger.

We would be reattuned to Tajss, living in harmony with the planet. The humans were the key. Our reward for the horrors we have survived and those that we caused. The weight of my past is crushing but it was all done to save Tajss.

She is my salvation. She tugs at my very soul, calling me to find her. When I do we will make the most beautiful, passionate love.

I'm barely aware of my hand on my cock, slowly stroking.

Our love burns brighter than both the suns of Tajss. When we are finally together the surviving planets of the Federation will know of our love because it is a supernova, waiting to happen. Even these Invaders might well retreat before the glory of that moment.

The dragon roars as I explode, finding some measure of relief. The aching need recedes enough that I will be able to sleep. I clean myself and lie down. Tomorrow. Tomorrow will be the day I find her, at last. She will be in my arms.

I'm coming, my love. My treasure.

GONG – CLANG – GONG – CLANG – GONG

"AAARGH!" Someone is roaring in rage outside my room.

I leap from my bed, eyes bleary, head ringing with the sounds of the alarm. Another scream echoes through my closed door. I throw the closest garment at hand over my head, the plain robe from my trip to the City, and throw the door open. A young warrior is running down the hall with fear etched into the scales of his face. Still, his eyes are hard and determined.

"What is this alarm?" I shout to be heard over the din.

"Invaders!" he says. "They're in the compound!"

"Impossible," I snap.

"Yes, s-s-si-sir," he stutters, trembling as he stops and comes to attention. "But they are."

I grab my lochaber from the wall rack. I haven't wielded my weapon in battle in more than a lifetime, but still the smooth wood is familiar. It settles into my hands like an old friend or the feel of my own cock.

"Where?" I ask. He points down the hall. I try to remember his name, but it doesn't come to me. I don't interact with the younger ones often enough to know them all on sight. "Follow me."

I take the lead, racing toward the danger. Invaders, in the compound? He has to be wrong. How did they breach our defenses? How did they get so close without setting off the alarms long before they reached the compound?

A subtle acrid scent fills my nostrils. Almost drowned out by the clanging of the alarms is a faint but familiar sound. I run faster down the hall, unable to believe it. I must be mistaken—it can't be what it sounds like.

We reach a door. I grab the handle and jerk my hand back in surprise. The handle is burning hot and my scales are seared.

Tendrils of smoke emerge from beneath the door like grasping fingers. I take a step back and push the warrior behind me. Then I kick the door with all I've got. It shatters beneath the impact, shards of wood exploding into the room beyond.

The now-open door is a window onto chaos.

Fire is climbing the walls of what was once a gathering room. Fallen, mangled bodies litter the floor. I'm agape at the horror before me but barely able to process the bodies. The war is here, raging inside our compound.

Four Invaders fill the room, massive monsters with their four arms, roaring their triumph. Wetness splashes onto my tail and the backs of my legs as the warrior behind me loses his stomach.

"Fight!" I yell, glancing back at him. "With me!"

I shift my grip on the lochaber and charge. My backup was pale faced and shaking, but his training kicks in and he is at my side. He swings his lochaber in a wide arc and I match it from the other angle. We split apart, moving around the massive post in the center of the room, avoiding the flames licking up to the ceiling.

We close on the opposite side of the post, finishing our swings. I adjust my swing, weaving it between the defensive weapons of my opponent. They all seem to have the same armaments. Swords in their upper two hands and heavy sticks with wicked-looking spikes sticking in all directions for the lower two.

My blade skids across the Invaders armor but I expected this. I twist the lochaber in my hands rotating the blade up and pull it up and back. It slides into a crease in his armor and bites into soft flesh, severing the tendons that control the arm.

9

My opponent roars, turning to face me directly. He swings three arms, weaving his weapons so fast they form a shield, and all I can do is parry and back away. Behind him I see the young warrior retreating before the onslaught of the one Invader.

Mirtan. His name's Mirtan. It comes to me, crazily, as I'm hard-pressed not to lose my head. Another of the Invaders joins the one already on me. I miss a parry and one of the clubs slams into my side. Crushing force that knocks my air out.

I'm thrown to the side, off balance. I drop to one knee dodging a blade and a club that would have taken off my head.

I swing my tail and connect with the newcomer's knee. There's a satisfying crunch as I connect and he stumbles, falling into his friend.

Jumping up I land lightly on my feet.

"Keep hope, Mirtan!" I yell. "Fight!"

Instantly I regret my words. Mirtan glances at me, and before I can speak again, the blade swinging for his neck connects. His eyes go wide as blood spurts, and then the light in them is gone.

My dragon roars and red covers my vision. His loss will not go unanswered.

I attack while the two are off balance. I whirl my lochaber up, around, swinging down, connecting with the blade side and the shaft. I stab the metal spike of the base into one of the Invaders.

I press the attack and my opponents fall back. With rage fueling my limbs, I rush them again, but the other two Invaders join them. Four against one are not odds any warrior should willingly face.

The red haze recedes. I take several steps back, returning to a defensive stance. They're used to working together as a team, and it shows. They move their weapons in unison, some keeping up a constant shield while other weapons attack.

I'm hit more than once as I keep retreating. This area is lost.

I glance at Mirtan's prone form and say a short prayer, passing his soul to Tajss.

I try to block an incoming blade but it's a feint and I take a club to the head. Stars fill my vision as I stumble backwards, swinging my lochaber wildly around to hold them at bay while I recover. When my vision clears, I'm almost back to the tunnel we entered from, almost where I need to be.

They form a semi-circle before me and are pressing in. I fall back, letting them think they have the advantage. When I cross the threshold back into the hall I smile.

"Tajss will never be yours," I growl.

I punch the wall of the hall to my left. The concealing panel falls away and I grab the lever, pulling it towards me.

The Invaders stop their advance, looking up as something rumbles and dirt falls on their head. An instant later, the stone ceiling collapses, burying them and Mirtan. Dirt and pebbles fill the air as I turn my back on the ruin and run.

The compound is lost. I have to reach the record room, activate the Invasion protocols, and then save as many as I can.

2

ANNA

BOOM!

"Wha--?" My head cracks against the floor as I'm tossed out of my bed and thrown awake. I snap my eyes open and sit up.

The ground rumbles under my butt and then there's another explosion. Dirt falls from the ceiling as I climb to my feet. I can hear shouting and cursing. The ground rocks, and I'm tossed from side to side as I make my way to the door of my room.

There's shouting and yelling on the other side of my door. Footsteps resound out there but stop at the same time as I touch the door handle. When I jerk the door open, I'm face-to-face with Petras. His tanned face is pale, his eyes wide, and he's showing too many teeth.

"What's happened?" I ask.

"Invaders," he says. His eyes are wide and he's shaking like a leaf in a storm.

"Again?" I ask. This isn't the first time we've fought them off.

"Worse," he says. "Come on."

I follow him into the hall, and the world tilts on its axis. I'm thrown against the wall and bite my tongue. Coppery blood touches my tongue. The boom is so loud my ears are ringing. I push myself upright and there's another explosion, throwing me to the opposite wall.

Dirt and debris pelt us from the ceiling. Ice-cold panic bursts through my body, taking control of my conscious thought until there is nothing but reactive instinct. Fear.

"Run!" I scream, grabbing at Petra's arm. "Out!"

Have to get out. Tunnels bad. Can't stay.

I'm stumbling forward as one explosion after another slams down. It's as if some titan from hell is using the mining shafts for his steel. Slamming a massive hammer onto our home over and over.

"Get out of my way," Petras screams, grabbing my arm and shoving me aside.

"Petras!" I yell at his retreating back.

The sound of my own voice is dim and distant, overridden by the ringing in my ears. I never liked him anyway. Asshole. Since Gershom died, he's been more of a jerk than ever. He's a die-hard anti-Zmaj douche.

"Screw you too!" I yell.

The ground keeps rumbling as more explosions come from above. I have to get out of the tunnels. I'm tossed from side to side as I run, bouncing off the walls. My blood runs cold when the sound of ringing steel is followed by a scream so high-pitched it can mean only one thing. They're inside the tunnels.

I skid to a stop, frozen. I thought I was scared before, but that was nothing. The sounds cut through the ringing in my ears. Another scream that's cut off short. This can't be...

Idiot, run!

I don't recognize the voice in my head but it's reasonable. Running is the best idea I've got. I turn around and run the opposite direction. The tunnels that we call home twist and turn around on each other. They were exhausted mine tunnels until we arrived and got to work.

The buildings on the surface would have been the expected housing for us but the heat was too much. None of us are taking epis, the body-altering plant of Tajss that makes it feasible for humans to survive here. I would, if there was any to take, but I could never tell the others that. I'd be chastised at best and outcast at worst.

We tried living in those buildings, but then Jacob and Phillip had the idea to move into the tunnels and make our homes under the ground. Away from the brutal double suns that bake Tajss every day.

I skid around another corner. There is loose dirt and debris on the floor, making it impossible to stop myself. The wall looms large, then I hit in a tangle of limbs.

"Anna!" someone yells.

I whirl around to see Phillip. Awkward. Nothing like running into your ex while also running for your life.

"Hey," I say.

Hey? Seriously, like it's any other day? What next, how's your love life without me?

"They're in the tunnels," he says.

"No shit?" I ask before I can stop myself.

The hurt is written so clearly on his face that I instantly feel bad. Sometimes I'm a bitch, but damn, someone stating the obvious is one of my biggest pet peeves.

"Have you seen Drosdan? Or Sarah?" he asks.

"Are you serious? You want a big bad Zmaj to save us now? Why would they? We treat them like shit. Besides, we don't need them. Come on, move!"

I grab his shoulders and force him to turn. He stumbles forward, and I keep pushing until we're both running. Having someone besides myself to focus on helps. The fear is a low hum, not letting me forget it's there, but not running the show either. At least for the moment.

"Where?" he asks.

Well he yells, since I wouldn't hear shit if he spoke in a normal voice. I poke my finger in my ear and twist hoping to make the ringing stop.

"Away," I answer. "And about Drosdan, I think he and Sarah went to the Tribe for supplies."

"Shit," he says.

"You're just full of good words and contradictions, aren't you?" I ask.

The explosions stop. A heavy silence falls. We're standing in a crossroads of four tunnels. I turn in a circle, the hair on the back of my neck standing on end and goose pimples racing up and down my arms.

"What does it mean?" Phillip asks.

I spare a fast glance for him before finishing my turn. The tunnels are empty at least as far as I can see. They're lit up with torches spaced out ever forty-five feet so I can't see much. Phillip grabs my arm in a death grip.

"Ouch!" I exclaim.

"What do we do?" he demands.

"How the hell do I know?" I snap. No wonder we didn't work out. Isn't he supposed to be the man? The one saving me? Ugh. "This way."

There are two choices, up to the surface or deeper into the mines. One glance at the ceiling was enough to leave my stomach quivering. There are fault lines running across it, and I'm relatively sure that before long, it's going to come down. No way I'm going to be stuck down here when it does.

"That's going up!" he screeches.

"Oh, really?" I ask.

"We can't go up, they're up there!"

"Newsflash, wonder boy, they're down here with us, too," I say. "So you want to be trapped in the tunnels with them, or out there where you at least have a chance to run?"

He nods and shuts his mouth. Look Ma, miracles do happen. I break into a run. As we pass a side tunnel, something moves.

I scream, leaping to one side.

Several people emerge from the tunnel. They're dirty and scared. I barely recognize them.

"I think I peed," I sigh, pressing a hand against my chest to keep my heart from breaking free.

"We have to get out of here," Jacob says. "Now."

"Seen any of the others?" I ask.

Jacob glances over his shoulder before answering. "Gone."

"Gone?" Phillip asks.

My stomach drops, leaving an empty, yawning pit. Cold seeps through my limbs and the hair on my arms tingles painfully.

"Everyone?" I ask.

"I'm not... sure," he says, "but we have to move, fast. They're not taking prisoners."

Clenching my hands and my jaw, I nod and lead the way forward. It isn't far before the tunnel ends at a ladder. Above is a heavy metal door. I put one hand on the ladder and stare up, straining to hear past the ringing that still hasn't gone away.

I look over my shoulder at the dozen pair of eyes staring at me. Me. No pressure. Facing the ladder, I close my eyes, inhale deeply, hold the breath, then let it out slowly. Here we go. One foot on the ladder and there's no turning back.

I reach the door and shift my position on the ladder so that I can press my ear against it. I wait for a count of ten, but all I hear is the high-pitched whine of my pissed-off eardrums. Everyone below is staring up at me, and I feel their stares like a weight on my soul. If I'm wrong, I'm not only killing myself, I'm killing all of us.

Right. Well, here goes nothing.

I grab the handle and twist to unlock it. It screeches in protest as the metal latch moves. My heart is racing, certain I've done it now. I wait for something, anything to happen, but nothing does. Letting out my held breath, I push the door up and... I'm staring up at an Invader's ass. He whirls around, weapons in each of his four hands, and glares.

"Hi," I say. "Passing through, do you mind?"

He growls, grunts, and makes a ticking, clicking sound. Could be language, could be an itch. He motions up with a club. I climb out of the hole and let the door slam back into place, with luck hiding the others. He pokes the club into my stomach, pushing me back, making more noises that I assume are words.

I raise my hands into the air. Damn, this thing is ugly. Four arms is not sexy. His skin is an icy blue, his eyes are a weak, washed out green, and his teeth are yellowed, yeah, how about, 'no thank you.'

"I'll be going now," I say, smiling and taking a step back. "Nice meeting you."

My stomach ties itself into knots as a wave of nausea hits hard, creating cold sweat on my face. The Invader is staring, but not moving, so I take another step back. Nothing. This is working, god knows why, but I'm going to move out, and then the others can slip out when these guys move on.

My heart is beating in staccato. My mouth is dry, and I'm too scared to breathe. One more step. Not taking my eyes off of the Invader, I attempt to process what I'm seeing in my peripheral vision. The stone buildings of the original mining settlement are to either side. Beyond them is empty, open desert, also known as escape. Or freedom. Hell, how about living? One more step and I'm bolting. Just one more, and I'll at least be outside of his reach. He'll have to run if he wants me, which apparently, he doesn't?

The corners of his lips curl. Screw it, I'm running. I spin on one foot and slam directly into the chest of another Invader.

I fall on my ass to the unmistakable sound of laughter. Who knew that one sound would be universal among so many species? So glad I'm here to find this out. I stare up at the new one, and he barks something then motions with all four arms. As if all of those motions and sounds mean something to me.

"Sorry," I say. "I don't speak asshole."

I give him my best eff-you smile then look to my left. The desert is so close, taunting. I guess there is something that could make me love that empty hellhole. It sure looks a lot better than being here with these two.

The one behind shoves something into my shoulder, hard. It hurts even though I move with the motion. I glare up and over at him, but he pushes again. There are metal spikes, sharp like nails, sticking out of the club he's pushing into me. Those are causing the pain.

I climb to my feet, slowly, trying to keep both of them in my vision. They say something one to the other, then there's more laughter. Great.

"Okay," I say, holding my hands up facing them. "You guys want this place, you can have it. I don't care, seriously. Haven't been a fan since I arrived. You can have the entire blasted planet for all I care."

The one on the right raises his upper arms that have a sword in each hand. The blades glint in the starlight. I'm frozen watching that shiny, sparkling edge slicing through the air towards me. Some tiny part of my brain is screaming to move, dodge, jump, do *something*, but that voice isn't reaching the control center.

My life flashes before my eyes. No, that's a lie. My regrets flash through my thoughts. One, my eyes never leave the blade that is about to shear me in two. Two, it's definitely not going so slow that I see my entire life.

Stupid moments is it. Moments I've never forgotten because of the pain. My first boyfriend. Telling my Mom I hated her. Agreeing to go on a 'date' with Phillip. Staying with Gershom because I was too scared to be alone.

Yeah, all my greatest hits flitting through my thoughts. All those moments I wish I could change. Won't be happening now, this blade is about to make sure of it.

"ARRGGHHH!"

The blade veers aside as something massive hits the wielder, tackling him directly into the other one.

I blink, then blink again, shaking, and this time I'm sure I peed myself, a little bit anyway.

The two Invaders are a tangle of limbs on the ground wrestling with one another. I stand frozen with fear, staring, mouth agape and waiting for my body to listen to me mentally screaming for it to obey. Too slowly, my mind processes the twisting mass of limbs on the ground.

"Drosdan?" my voice squeaks.

Drosdan is one of the few Zmaj who ever comes to our camp, because of Sarah. Drosdan has one of the Invaders by the throat pinning him down on top of the other one. They're swinging wildly all eight of their arms, one of which is holding a club and another holding a sword. Drosdan glances over.

"RUN!" he hisses through gritted teeth.

I hate to admit it, but his command breaks through my paralysis. As fast as thought, I'm running away from the fight. I make it to the edge of the first building when another realization sends me skidding to a stop, and I spin back around.

Drosdan and the Invaders are wrestling on the ground. Drosdan is big. When I say big, I mean really, really big. Zmaj

19

are all huge, really, averaging around seven feet tall and all built as if they are competitors for the universe's strongest man. Drosdan, though, is big compared to other Zmaj.

His shoulders are so wide I think I could stretch out on them and take a nap. His biceps are as big as my waist and his fists are the size of my head. How he and Sarah ever make it together makes no sense. Great! Random thoughts when lives are at stake.

The two Invaders seem to be getting the better of Drosdan despite his size. They're not as big as he is, but they're close. And there are two of them. The three of them are rolling around in the sand, then one of them ends up on top of Drosdan, and the other slams a club into Drosdan's head.

CRUNCH!

Acid climbs my throat as my stomach clenches tight at the sound. Drosdan howls in pain and blood is pouring from the newly opened wound. I have to help. Somehow. Desperate, I look around for anything I can use as a weapon.

The night is suddenly alight as a pillar of flame climbs skyward from one of the buildings. It looks like a flaming finger, telling the gods above where they can shove it. I raise an arm shielding my eyes from the flames. Heat rushes across my exposed skin, blistering hot.

Something sparkles out of the corner of my eye. I run towards it, hoping against hope it will be something useful. The afterimage of the flames is making it hard to see, so I drop to my knees and feel my way towards the sparkle.

My hand touches something cooler and harder than the sand. I close my fingers around a wooden shaft. I tighten my grip with my left hand and run my right hand down it as I lift. A lochaber! The chosen weapon of the Zmaj. A long shaft with a sharp, pointed blade mounted on the top and the bottom is a metal-cased point.

I leap to my feet, lochaber gripped in both hands. The after-image is clearing from my eyes, but I wish it weren't. Drosdan is in serious trouble. He's swinging wildly with fists and tail. He's struggling to get to his feet but one of the Invaders is holding his legs while the other has backed away and retrieved his weapons.

None of them are paying attention to me, so I run wide around them. When I get behind the one stalking Drosdan with the weapons, I lower the lochaber, pointing the sharp blade at the Invader's back. I charge.

When I'm almost to him, I close my eyes and turn my head. Everything happens at once. The blade hits the Invader, sending a shockwave up my arms causing them both to go numb. The Invader screams, but it's cut short and he drops, jerking the lochaber out of my numb hands.

I open my eyes a crack and see Drosdan throw the one on top of him up into the air. The Invader's arms and legs flail and he yells. Drosdan pushes off the ground with his tail and as he rises up, he swings one mighty fist in front of himself. That fist connects with the Invader's jaw who then flips over, blood flying, and lands on his back with a thud.

Drosdan slams his tail onto the Invader's chest as he closes the distance, then drops down and pounds the Invader over and over. The Invader is lifeless beneath Drosdan's raging attack. His head is lolling back and forth under the onslaught.

I open my eyes the rest of the way, and only then am I aware of the slick blood covering my hands and chest. My stomach rebels, I turn my head and lose my dinner. Drosdan grabs my shoulders and spins me to face him.

"Okay?" he asks in Common.

"Yes," I nod, wiping my sleeve across my mouth. "Yeah."

"Run," he says, pointing out into the desert.

He whirls and the last I see of him is as he runs past a burning building towards shadowy figures outlined with the

21

flames like demons from some abyssal hell. I'm not going to waste the chance he bought for me. I rush to the trap door and throw it open. Yelps echo up the tunnel and scrambling.

"It's me," I say. "Come on!"

I stand watch as they climb out. Jacob emerges last and we all stand in a huddle. I should be feeling something, but I don't. I'm staring at the destruction of the life we've built, and I've got nothing. I'm not even sure I'm awake. This all feels like it's happening to someone else.

"What now?" Phillips asks.

"Run," I say.

"Where?" he asks.

Everyone is looking at me as if I have all the answers. Right, I've got jack and shit folks. I'm still trying to figure out if this is a nightmare brought on by some bad guster meat.

"The City," I say.

"We can't go there," Petras says. "Rosalind hates us."

"You got a better idea?" I snap, stepping into his personal space and glaring him down.

He meets my glare with one of his own, jaw clenching tight. The group forms a circle around us. Once again, I should be scared, or backing down, or reacting in some way. I'm not even angry. Irritated maybe, but not what I would call angry. I'm not really here after all, this is a nightmare so I can do what I want.

"No," he says, dropping his eyes and taking a small step back.

"Good, now move," I say pointing out into the desert.

No one argues further and we break into a run. The heat of our burning homes warms our backs as we run. Everything we've known, all our work, gone. In a heartbeat. Damn, I hate this place.

3

KHABRI

THICK SMOKE COVERS THE FLOOR OF THE HALL, RISING TO MY knees. The acrid scents of burning wood, paper, and flesh assault my senses, stinging my eyes and nose. Sounds of battle drift through the air, but I don't encounter anyone in this tunnel.

This is one of the many hidden passages that riddle the compound. I run as fast as I can until I come to a blank wall. I press my hands against the surface, checking for heat. It is cool to the touch, so I press my ear to it, listening. Nothing.

Now I open it and slip through, being careful to remember to slide it closed behind me. The hall I've entered runs in either direction about ten strides. Fighting echoes from both directions, but my goal is right in front of me. I step across the hall and open the door to the Records Room.

This door looks like wood, but the wood is a façade covering thick steel. Looking both ways first, I close the door, then slide the bar across it to lock myself in. The room smells of old paper and leather. As valuable as these old scrolls are, they are not of the highest value. I stride past them to the back of the room and run my hands over the blank, smooth wall there.

When I find the latch, I apply pressure, and a section of the wall lowers itself out, revealing the real treasure. A series of crystals lines the table thus revealed. The true records of the Order. Our memory of all that has come and of every prediction the Eye has made.

This cannot fall into enemy hands. I drift my hand across them, steeling my nerve for what I am going to do. Suddenly my dragon roars to life, and I'm blinded with an unthinking rage. My vision shifts and I'm no longer looking at the crystals, but at an Invader. He stares, and I'm aware of fear. Fear that isn't mine.

Her. She's in danger. Protect her.

I shake with unbridled anger, but there is nothing I can do. My mate is in danger. I've yet to lay eyes on her, but I know it. I know this vision is true, though I've never before been granted the sight.

I slam my fists down on the crystals. They explode under the force of my blows. The wood of the table itself cracks and splinters. I slam them again and again, destroying the entire apparatus. Still my rage is untamed.

Instinct rages to protect, to save her, but there is nothing I can do. I roar as I rampage, destroying the room.

The vision fades away. I'm left standing in the wake of my own destruction, shaking in the aftermath of my own anger. A hidden door slides open, and three Zmaj burst into the room.

"Councilor!" Aeros exclaims, seeing me.

The three of them look around, shock obvious on their faces.

"Destruction protocols," I say, forcing my emotions under control. "Now!" I bark when none of them move.

They snap to attention and set to work. The males jump at my command, but not before their eyes widen and their tails stiffen. Two males gather scrolls and papers into a pile. Aeros stomps on the mangled crystals, finishing the work I started.

As each crystal crunches my stomach knots and bile rises in my throat. We are destroying our memory. The only records of

Tajss I know for sure still exist. Tajss from before the Devastation. My beloved planet and its history—but the past is a weapon that must not fall into these Invaders' hands.

"Has anyone seen the Premier?" I ask.

"No, sir," Typhon answers. "We'd hoped he was here."

"How far have they penetrated?" I ask.

The three warriors pause and look at each other before anyone answers.

"Almost all the way," Pachua says.

"How did this happen?" I ask.

"They seem to have disabled the early alarms," Reoz says.

"Impossible," I mutter, shaking my head.

They don't contradict me, but I know I'm lying to myself since obviously they did. Pachua kneels next to the piles of papers and books and belches flame. Fire licks hungrily at the dry tinder and in moments it's clawing its way across the pile. The four of us step back, standing side-by-side watching our life's work burn.

The sense of loss in my guts tears at me, but there is something more important. My mate is out there, on this planet, and obviously the Invaders aren't holding back. I must find her.

"What does this mean, sir?" Reoz asks.

I stare into the flames, letting the warmth soak into my scales.

"That Tajss has been put back into play," I say.

"Play, sir?" Pachua asks.

I turn my head and stare until his scales color with shame.

"Have you learned nothing? Do you not do your studies?" I ask.

"Sir... I mean...," he looks past me at the door to the records room.

"I know," I say, shaking my head. "How many lost?"

"Most, sir," Pachua says softly.

"Your brother?" I ask, not wanting to know the answer.

Pachua and his brother were almost as inseparable as Archion and Khal, more even. They were the only twins in our compound. Often finishing one another's sentences, even.

"I do not know," he says, his twitching hands and tail showing his agitation.

"They're Invaders," I say. "Invaders are cloned soldiers, war-meat, that means someone on one of the other planets has gone from suspecting epis exists on Tajss to knowing it. If they're launching a full-scale invasion, as it seems, then every Zmaj and Human on the planet is in trouble. It's up to us to save them all," I say.

"Yes, sir," the three males answer as one.

"It's on us," I say. "One way or another."

They nod their acceptance of the reality.

"Even if?" Aeros asks.

"Yes," I answer, knowing what he's asking without it having to be said. "Even as we did before. If it comes to that, we will activate the Devastation protocols."

The only sound is the crackling fire as it consumes history, hungry still and more than willing to consume the future as well. Fire lives in the moment. No past, no future, it rages until there is nothing left, and it sputters out. I can only hope that it's not a metaphor for us.

"Separate, find as many as you can," I order. "Gather them and escape. We'll meet at the Weeping Male rock. You all know it?"

They nod that they do and then we separate into the halls. I grab Aeros by the arm before he heads off.

"Stay with me," I order.

I lead the way towards the Council Chamber area. It's deep in our compound, and I hope that some have taken refuge there, especially the Premier. This deep in the compound, the halls are wide enough for two Zmaj to walk abreast, but I let Aeros stay slightly ahead. The knowledge I have must survive.

The sounds of fighting are a constant din, accenting the clanging alarms that have not yet been shut down. There's so much noise I can't orient by sound. As we turn a corner we step into a battle.

Four Invaders block the hall, but backs are to us. My brethren are fighting the front two. The two in back stand ready to take advantage of any opening or to replace the fallen. Aeros doesn't hesitate, driving his lochaber into the back of the neck of one, and I mimic his motion on another before he can turn around.

They drop without a cry, but one of the others turns to face us. He whirls swords and clubs in all four hands. They whistle through the air forming an effective shield. Aeros stabs, feinting, probing for an opening. I step up and do the same. We alternate going high, low, instinctively doing the opposite of each other.

The Invader knocks the blades aside each time, keeping us from getting through. A grin spreads across his face, showing his yellowed teeth. He changes the pattern of his swings, moving from defensive to offensive. The two clubs continue a swirling dance but now the swords dart in and out like the tongue of a zmeya.

Aeros is nicked on the arm, grunting as the blade slices him. He steps back and the Invader advances, a blade jabbing at my left. I knock it aside but have to jump back too to avoid the other blade driving into my right.

I step on one of the bodies and my ankle twists. I stumble back, raising my lochaber in blind protection as I struggle to catch my balance. The blades swing in and out faster than I can follow, so I'm forced back more.

Aeros leaps to my aid. His lochaber blurs as he blocks blow after blow. I catch my balance and rush forward, but it happens

27

too fast. Aeros misses the block on an incoming club. It connects with his head, crushing it.

I avenge him with the opening thus created, driving my blade into the Invader's chest and then pulling up with a roar of rage. The blade slices through until it hits bone. I jerk it free, blood spraying.

The other Invader is overwhelmed now that it is two on one. No matter the clanging of the alarms that continue to ring, a heavy silence lies over us. I lean on my lochaber panting, eyes resting on Aeros.

He was a good warrior, a fine soldier. They all are. No member of the Order has ever been anything less than dedicated to our cause. Laying our lives on the line for the future of Tajss itself. He died serving the higher purpose.

"Sir," one of the other warriors says. I look up and recognize Vae and Palax. "We must move. There are more."

"A lot more," Palax says.

"Have you seen the Premiere?" I ask. They exchange a look that tells me all I need to know without them having to say it. "Others?"

"No, sir," Vae says.

"Right," I nod. "We need to escape. The compound is lost."

My chest clamps tight and my hearts struggle against the pressure. The look on the two warriors' faces mirrors the one I imagine is on my own. No matter, we have protocols in place for such a possibility, though none of us expected to ever use them.

I take the lead, racing through the smoke-filled halls. Bodies litter the floor. Our fallen brethren. The Invaders seem to be systematically hunting and killing us. This isn't a battle, it's an extermination.

Chilling fingers run along my spine and my wings flutter in response. They intend to take Tajss, and that must not happen.

I turn a corner and lead the way to a dead end. After running my hands over the wall, I find the trigger and open a hidden passage. This one is rough-hewn stone, cut through the rocky protrusion that hides the compound. I step to one side and usher the others into the tunnel before closing the door behind us.

"Follow the tunnel," I say.

It's dirty and tight. Dust and sand drift from the ceiling as we make our way through the stone tunnel until at last, we emerge onto the open sands. When I climb out of the trap door, I turn and look back. Flames soar out of the compound, revealing its hidden location to all. The flames climb so high and are so bright, I'm sure they can be seen from space. It looks as if someone has lit a signal fire for the gods themselves.

My vision blurs and doubles. I'm seeing two scenes at once, but they don't match. Reflexively, my hands clench into fists as fear clamps around my chest. All I've known is lost, and it's going to take all my will and power to make sure we don't lose Tajss in the process. It would be enough to fight for the planet, but it's not all I'm fighting to save.

Her.

She's out there, and she too is in danger. I'm seeing her home burn too. When I close my eyes, I still see the burning buildings. She turns away, taking the sight away, and I lose the tenuous connection, but not before I think I recognize the sight.

"Mining settlement," I whisper.

"Sir?" Vae asks.

I snap my eyes open, locking my gaze on him.

"Have you been to the humans' mining settlement?" I ask.

"No, sir," he says.

Frowning, I nod.

"I've been close to it, sir," Palax says.

"Describe it to me," I order.

The confusion is obvious on his face, but he's well trained and doesn't question. He gives a cursory, battlefield-style report of what he saw. He was never inside of the camp, spying on it from a distance only but it's enough. That is where she was.

"No wonder," I say.

"Sir?" Palax asks.

"Nothing," I snap. "We must reach the Weeping Male. Go."

We run across the desert to regroup with the others, but now I know why I haven't been able to find her. She was never in the City or at the Tribe's cave. She was out there, at the mining settlement. How did I never think of it?

Fate. It must be the guiding hand of Tajss itself, not letting us come together before it is time. As difficult as it is, my prime cock throbbing with desire for her, I must put my trust in Tajss. I will find her. She is closer now than ever before.

She is mine. It is only a matter of time.

4

LADON

"Come here," I growl, grabbing Calista's leg and jerking her across our bed.

She laughs as she struggles. "Ladon! Illadon will be up any moment."

"He's not yet," I say, kissing her shoulder.

The sheets have pulled down, revealing the tantalizing lines of her neck and the swell of her breasts.

"He will be," she says, shuddering as I continue trailing kisses along her exposed skin.

"In time," I agree. "You are the most beautiful female in the universe."

She stops resisting my attention, rolling towards me and throwing a leg over my hip.

"Oh?" she asks.

"Yes," I say. "You are perfect."

"I don't know about all that," she says, looking down.

I cup her cheek and draw her face back up to meet mine. Gazing into her perfect, brown eyes, I touch my lips to hers. Soft, gentle, brushing against her plushness. She shivers so I grab the treated furs we use for blankets and pull them up over us.

"Are you calling me a liar?" I ask.

"More biased," she says.

I trail my fingers through her hair, down on to her back and slide it under the sheet, exploring her exotically soft skin.

"Mine," I growl, hooking her ass and pressing her against me.

My prime cock digs into her stomach. She caresses my cheek, tilting her head back, welcoming my kiss. I absorb her body's heat, her heat burns against me, the fire that burns in my soul. She is all I've ever dreamed of.

The dragon rumbles in satisfaction. She is all I ever need or want.

"Yours," she whispers.

The dragon roars, satisfaction erupting into pleasure. Her submission creates such pleasure.

"Bury myself in you," I growl.

Rolling on top of her. The sheets try to stop my progress, so I rip them off the bed and throw them while shifting my hips. My cock is between her legs, pressing against her, ready to drive deep.

She spreads her legs, her lips part, her eyes closed. Ready to take me, offering herself to me.

I thrust, hard. Driving in, to the hilt. She gasps then exclaims as I fully seat myself inside of her, and my knob rubs hard on her clit.

Her hands claw across my back. She thrusts her hips up, quivering beneath me. I retreat slow. Experiencing every inch of my member sliding through her warm embrace. Pulling back until the tip is barely inside.

I hold, preparing my next thrust.

CRASH!

The sound of shattering glass from the next room stops me. Calista pushes me off and leaps from the bed. In a single motion she grabs the sheet from the floor and wraps it around herself as she races for the door.

I drop onto the bed, crushing my throbbing cock into the mattress. I roll over and groan, the blanket covering my middle tenting up still. Slamming my fists onto the bed, I curse silently.

"Sorry, Mommy," Illadon's voice says.

I love my son. He is as great a treasure as Calista, but damn his timing. Could he not sleep a bit longer? Is there nothing even in my own home I'm able to control? A few moments alone with his mother is all I wanted.

"It's fine," Calista says, but I hear the exasperation in her voice.

I grit my teeth, ball my hands in the sheets, then roll over and climb out of bed. My pants aren't where I left them. Anger flashes hotly across my vision, and I do my best to tamp it down. I look around the room, but nothing.

I toss aside discarded clothes and finally find them up under the bed frame. When I pull them on, my cock is still hard, but now my son is up. Calista won't help with it, because her attention will be tied up with Illadon.

Maybe Sverre and Jolie would have a play date? That might buy us an hour or two of alone time. Alone time, a distant memory.

I wish I'd never agreed to let all her 'friends' move into my City. How much simpler would our lives be if it were only the three of us?

The room is a mess and I need to take my mind off my throbbing dick, so I work to set it to rights. I pick up the discarded clothing, Calista's, as I only own two pairs of pants, and even that seems excessive. When I walk out with an armload of laundry, Calista is in our kitchen preparing food for Illadon.

"What broke?" I ask.

"Morning, Daddy!" Illadon says excitedly. "I was making breakfast. I was doing great. It was going to be perfect. I wanted to serve you breakfast in bed. The pitcher was slick, though. Sorry, it slipped. Now Mommy says I can't make breakfast for you. Or me either, I guess. This sucks, I'm able to. I can do anything I set my mind to."

I walk over to my son balancing the fine line between anger and pride. If nothing else, my cock isn't dominating my thoughts any longer.

I tousle his hair and tug his head around by grabbing his horns. He laughs and struggles against my wrestling.

"It's fine," I say.

I look to Calista and instantly my cock stiffens. She's so beautiful. Her long hair is tousled, sticking out in wild places, bunching around her perfect face. The sheet she's wearing is slowly slipping lower, barely covering the soft brown nipples that top her heavy breasts.

Have they gotten bigger? A little?

She looks up and gives me a wan smile, shaking her head. "I'll need to craft a new pitcher."

I nod my agreement and go to put the laundry in the woven basket she's made for the purpose of holding the items that need cleaned. I stare at the wrinkled pile of clothes in the basket. Neat. Organized. In its place.

A place for everything. It's satisfying.

When I turn around, I examine the living space. Toys and random objects lie strewn about, destruction in the path of my son's flittering attention. I deliberately walk around the room and pick up each out-of-place thing, firmly putting it back where it belongs. When I finish, I walk over to Illadon who is taking the last bites of his breakfast.

The counter around his plate is littered with crumbs, beads of water where he's spilt his drink, and dirt. I stare at the offending mess then look at my son.

"Illadon," I say. "You are making a mess. A male should take care of his own area. Do you expect your mother and me to clean up after you?"

Illadon stops chewing and looks at me with wide eyes. He shakes his head back and forth but doesn't speak. Calista stops what she is doing and turns back to us.

"Then clean it up," I bark, pointing at the mess around his plate.

"Yes, Daddy," he says, his voice soft, eyes no longer meeting mine.

He sets down his food and slides off the stool, walking into the kitchen to retrieve a rag.

"It's fine, Illadon, I'll get it," Calista says.

"No," I say, glaring at my treasure. "He must learn to care for himself. He can contribute to keeping our home in order."

"He can," she says, stepping towards me and placing a hand on her hip. "But he will do so because he wants to, not because you're controlling him."

"There is *nothing* wrong with control," I growl.

Calista opens her mouth to say something more, but she stops herself and snaps her mouth shut instead. She tilts her head, eyes narrowing as she studies me. She closes the distance until she has one hand on my chest and the other cupping my cheek.

"Ladon, what is it?" she asks.

Illadon is behind the counter dividing the kitchen area but I see him peek around the corner watching with blatant curiosity.

"I want to help you," I say. "Order, control, these are good things."

"Yes," she says. "But this isn't like you."

I stop myself from a fiery retort. Her hands are warm against my scales, so I focus on those and breathe. The bijass is still close to the surface. Anger comes too quickly, but it's more than that, isn't it?

"I don't know," I say.

"My love," she whispers. "If you don't know, what is it you feel?"

"Danger," I say, exploring the sensations and feelings that won't form into words. "As if we're on the precipice of something terrible."

"Is it the disease?" she asks.

"No," I snap. "It's not what was, it's something coming."

"Okay," she says.

"Let's leave," I say suddenly. "Now. Pack our things and go."

"We can't go," she says.

"Why not? What holds us here? I will make a life for you and for Illadon far from here. It's the way it should be, we don't belong here in this dead husk of a City. This isn't natural."

"Ladon," she says, shaking her head. "You're not yourself. It's probably unrest and upset from the illness. That's all. We're all fine. The City is great and we're getting better all the time."

I grab her arms and squeeze, trying to force her to understand.

"No!" I say. "It's not. We need to… leave. All these people, Rosalind, Visidion, deciding what we'll do next, what's important and what's not. This isn't right. We can go."

"I'm not leaving here," she says, defiantly jerking herself out of my grip and taking a step back.

Her face is clouded with anger, her head tilted up, lips pursed tight. She meets my glare with one of her own, staring me down. The dragon rumbles but I can't force her to understand. Anger burns through my veins, but there's nothing more I can do or say.

"Calista, please," I say, trying the one path left open.

"No," she says, shaking her head. "All our friends are here. Our families are here. I'm not leaving them for a feeling you have. I'm sorry, I love you Ladon, but no."

An emptiness opens up in my soul, and it feels like I'm being pulled towards a destiny we're not prepared to face. Something terrible is going to happen. I have to protect my family. How do I make her understand?

"Then we must prepare for war," I snap in anger.

"Ladon, we haven't even seen the Invaders in weeks," she says.

"You think that means they're gone?"

"Maybe? Maybe they got what they wanted and left," she says.

"Don't play a fool Calista, you're too smart for it," I say.

"Don't call me a fool," she says, eyes flashing in anger.

I bite my tongue as I struggle against the surging bijass.

Run. Take them. Run. No time. Protect. Care for.

It takes all my will to hold the red haze of primal instinct at bay. It creeps in around my control, urging, as it fights for control. Her resistance taunts it, daring her to continue. I will do what I must to protect my family.

"We must make a final strike," I say. "Now."

I can't stand here any longer. Since the illness it's been harder than ever to control the bijass. Fighting with her isn't helping. I stride to the front door.

"Don't you leave," she orders.

I look over my shoulder, one hand on the door.

"I love you," I say. Then I leave.

5

ANNA

I'VE LOST FEELING IN MY FEET. CORRECTION—I'VE LOST feeling everywhere. My nightmare isn't stopping. It goes on and on and on. Phillip stumbles and falls. His arms shake as he pushes himself up out of the sand.

Petras and I try to help him to his feet, but my arms are too heavy. I can't help. I can barely keep myself up. Some of the others come and help, and it takes a massive team effort, but we get him on his feet. He's weaving on his feet, his face blank and his eyes empty.

"Phillip," I say.

He doesn't respond. He doesn't even blink. I snap my fingers in front of his face, but nothing. I look at Petras and Jacob who each shrug in turn. I close my eyes and shake my head, a desperate attempt to clear my thoughts. Every thought comes slow, fighting its way through the thick tar that fills my head.

"Come on, Phillip!" Petras yells. Well he raises his voice, but I wouldn't call it a yell. A yell would take a lot more energy than any of us have left.

"Screw it," I say and slap Phillip across the face.

He yelps, eyes blinking as his hand flies to his cheek.

"Hey! What was that?" he asks, blissfully unaware we've been trying to get him to pay attention for the past ten minutes.

"You spaced," I say, ignoring the wriggle of pleasure the slap caused me.

He really hurt me when we were dating. The slap wasn't undeserved. After all, he cheated on me.

"Oh," he says, shaking himself. "Sorry."

"Be sorry later," Petras snaps. "Keep moving."

Phillip nods and stumbles into motion. The rest of the group follows suit. Fourteen. Fourteen of over a hundred. When I glance over my shoulder, there is a fitful orange glow on the horizon, brightening the night.

Our home. Or what was our home. That's over now, and once more the future is uncertain. I'm not the only one who keeps looking over my shoulder. Everyone is doing it.

"Why?" Maeve asks, tears streaming down her face.

Maeve looks rough, but I imagine it's a mirror of how I look. Soot stains mar her high cheekbones. Her dark eyes glitter with unshed tears. A hot breeze tugs her auburn hair away from her face. She wipes her sleeve across her eyes.

"I don't know," I say.

"Because somewhere, someone out there," Morgana points to the sky above, "really hates us."

Morgana is tall, curvy and busty. She has a strong face and sharp, intelligent eyes. She's the settlement's spiritualist. Often saying things like this, placing blame on some external force. She's starry-eyed, and I've never liked her myself. I don't hate her, but she has a weird vibe and makes me feel like she's looking through me, not at me. It's creepy.

"Thanks for that helpful input," I snark.

I can't put any force behind the quip. That would require me to feel something.

"Anyone have anything to eat?" Sophia asks.

Sophia is short—she barely comes up to my tits. Her face is so cute it hurts, framed by pure blonde hair and bright eyes. Her skin is flawless. She reminds me of a porcelain doll. When she smiles it warms my heart but she's not smiling now. How could she?

"I have some meats," Liam says, holding up a leather satchel.

The group looks to me. How I became the de facto leader is beyond me. They obviously don't know I'm as clueless as anyone. I shrug and nod my assent. Everyone gathers around into a loose huddle as Liam digs into the bag and passes out pieces of smoked meat.

I take one myself and chew the leathery meat. It helps ease the pounding headache, a little at least. No one talks. Everyone is staring at the ground. Emptiness pulses in time with my heartbeat.

"We need to keep moving," I say, swallowing the last of my share.

My throat is dry and raw. I work my mouth trying to force out some moisture, but it doesn't help. I know we're all feeling the same. We didn't have time to prepare for a journey across the desert. No water. The fact we have food at all is a lucky break.

We're a small mob, stumbling across the sandy dunes. I'm not even sure we're going in the right direction. I think so. I hope so. It's hard to focus. One moment blends with the next as my thoughts drift randomly. Sometimes I think I skip time. At least I'm not aware of it passing when I'll suddenly realize my surroundings are completely different. Progress, right?

Random pictures flash through my thoughts. Horrible scenes of those we've lost. Sometimes my stomach tightens, and bile threatens my throat. If there was anything in my stomach to lose, I'm sure it would be gone. As it is, I'm only miserable.

"Fuck Gershom," Emma yells, startling me. She shakes her fist at the sky, tears streaming down her face. "Fuck you!"

"Emma," I say, but I don't stop stumbling forward. My feet are on a mission and they're not going to be stopped by minor inconveniences. "It's okay."

"No, it's not!" she yells, stumbling in my direction.

She's flushed, teeth bared, the dirt marring the dark skin of her face gives her a wild, primal look. The way her eyes flash in the moonlight would probably be scary if it could pierce past the armor of numbness that's wrapped itself around my soul.

"I agree," Jacob says. "Fuck him."

Some instinct in me wants to argue yet it's not like I care. Gershom was a liar. A false messiah. Or, colloquially, an asshole. All his Human First rhetoric turned out to be nothing more than a blatant power grab.

He preyed on our fears, insecurities, and need for hope, any hope for a future. That we would all survive this, somehow. He's the one who preached no epis. No depending on the Zmaj, telling us that we should be in control, not them. That they were evil, more or less, and plotting our downfall.

I never bought it, at least not all of it. Yet I was as scared as anyone. How could I be anything else? We'd survived the crash of the generation ship that was the only home we had ever known. The only home we'd ever expected to see. When Calista hooked up with one of the seven-foot-tall alien dragon men it seemed wrong.

When more of the aliens showed up, we all thought it was planned. That's not true, we were told it was planned. I didn't know and honestly didn't care, but I did find them scary. They're so big and different. What could I do to stop one of those alien men from doing whatever he wanted?

Mostly, all my friends were following Gershom and it was

easier to go along. I didn't want to be alone. Alone was the worst.

"Should have taken epis," Aurora grouches. "Least then I'd not feel like death warmed over."

"Right?" Emma asks. "Why did we listen to him? He *lied* to us! He was taking epis the entire time and it fucking killed him."

"He got what he deserved," Jacob says.

"Karma," Morgana agrees.

I roll my eyes. Karma. Right, some grand design of the universe making sure bad people get what's coming to them. As if.

Something tugs at my attention, but I can't put my finger on it. I stop walking and turn in a slow circle. The group comes to a stop around me.

"What is it?" Eloise asks.

I don't answer, holding a finger up to my lips. Something, outside the shield of numbness, past the throbbing aches and pains. My feet?

I kneel and place my palm on the hot, rough sand. The individual grains are sharp and pokey. Uncomfortably so. I close my eyes and wait, focusing my awareness.

Vibrations.

"Shit, run!" I yell, springing upright and spinning back the direction we were going.

"What is it?" a chorus of voices ask.

"Run! They're coming after us!" I yell.

Yelps and soft screams, but everyone is running. We must look like idiots to anyone watching this from a distance. A shambling horde. Zombies. We look like zombies stumbling across an empty desert.

We run until the group begins spreading out, the slower ones falling behind, unable to keep up. We're halfway up yet another dune when Christine, who is next to me, stumbles and falls on her face. I reach for her, but before I can catch her, she's sliding down the hill.

"Catch her!" I yell.

Hilarity ensues as dozens of hands try to catch her, and she tries to stop herself. Well, it would be hilarious if we weren't running for our lives. It's not funny right now. It's terrifying, but the terror lives outside my protective shell.

Nope, here inside my bubble, life is totally fine. I don't feel a thing. Petras, of all people, catches the back of Christine's shirt and though he slides a few more feet down they come to a stop. She climbs to her feet, shaking.

"Are you okay?" I ask.

She dusts herself off before looking up the hill to me and nodding. Her eyes are sunken, shoulders stooped, and tears glitter on her light-brown cheeks.

I let the group trudge past me. No one is running now. They're too worn out, and without an immediate, obvious threat I don't know how to encourage them. Staring into the darkness of the night, I debate what to do next.

The vibrations I felt are definitely vehicles, but are they looking for us? Do they care? It's not like we're a threat. A handful of humans who are barely able to survive on this shit-hole planet. What threat do we pose?

None, but then what threat did we pose living in our comfortable tunnels and doing a bit of mining? Why did they decide to destroy our home? There's more going on here than I have the brain to process. Morgana trudges up the hill and comes to a stop at my side. Great. If there is a universal intelligence guiding all of this, it hates me.

"It won't be long," she says ominously.

"Until?" I ask.

"They're looking for us," she says. "I can feel their intention."

"You can 'feel their intention?'" I ask unable to keep my voice from raising.

"Of course," she says, either deliberately ignoring my disbelieving tone or oblivious to it.

A thousand retorts flash across my thoughts, each snarkier and meaner than the last. Finally I settle on an exhausted sigh. I don't have the energy to waste on her.

"We need to keep moving," I say. "The City is this way."

"Our next target is the Oasis," Morgana says without moving.

"What are you talking about?" I ask, not bothering to turn around.

"We need to reach the Oasis," she says. "That is the next point of convergence."

"The next point of convergence," I mutter. "Of course, what was I thinking."

Morgana flashes a brilliant, bright smile then moves past me. I follow in her wake, wishing against all hope that I knew what the right thing to do was. She's talking about an Oasis, and I have no idea if such a thing even exists.

No, wait. There was one not far from the wreckage of the ship. I never went there, but I remember Gershom had people go there for water and wood when we were first exiled. Back before we all found out he was taking epis without telling anybody. He died of the withdrawals when Rosalind exiled him and those of us stupid enough to follow him.

I was an idiot. I don't know where the Oasis is though, and Morgana seems to. I speed up coming down the far side of the dune trying to catch up to her. When I'm next to her I match her pace.

"Where?" I ask.

"Hmm?"

"Where is this Oasis?" I ask. "Are we going in the right direction?"

"Of course we are," she says. "Fate is drawing us there like a leaf on the current of a rushing river."

I barely stop my eyes from completing the full roll.

"There is no such thing as fate," I say. "Do you know the actual way to the Oasis or not?" Morgana smiles and laughs but she doesn't answer.

"Morgana!" Others look over their shoulders at us. I drop my voice. "Do you know a way or not?"

I'm hissing. I don't want to be, I feel like an idiot. All this mysticism and talk of fate sounds like bullshit to me.

"Sometimes," Morgana says. "You have to put your faith in something more."

"Still not an answer," I bite off each word.

"No, but it's the best I can give you," she says. "I know it's not the answer you seek, but perhaps it's the answer you need."

"Do you practice this?" I ask, waving my hand up and down her.

"This?" she asks, furrowing her brow.

"The whole I'm a creepy seer who knows something you don't know thing?"

"No."

Exhaustion hits me like a wave in the ocean and I come to a stop. It swells over, pulling me under, and I'm left with nothing. I take a deep breath and hold it, then let it out in a rush.

"Sorry," I say. "I'm being a bitch."

"It's fine," Morgana says. She moves closer and places her hand on my arm. "I understand."

She does, too. It's in her eyes, written across the kindness on her face, in the warmth of her touch. My eyes burn, stinging with regret and loss trying to break through my blanket of numb.

Outside my shell, a hurricane of unwanted emotions rages, but there isn't time for it. Not now, maybe not ever.

"We need to move," I choke out.

"Yes," Morgana says, but she doesn't step away. Instead she steps closer and wraps her arms around me, squeezing me tight.

I feel it, see it happening, but I'm standing stock-still. It's as if it's happening to someone besides me. Awkward doesn't describe it. I raise my arms and return the hug, and then she steps back, keeping a grip on both of my arms. She kisses my left cheek, then my right.

"Tajss bless you," she whispers.

"Uhm, thank you," I say.

I've got no clue how to respond to this. It's beyond the weird. How did she end up out there with us at the Mining colony? Seems like she would fit in with the Tribe or the City much better. She seems satisfied with my answer, and we resume our journey.

At the crest of the next dune, I pause and study the landscape. The moon and stars cast a soft silvery light across the desert. It's beautiful when it looks like this and the planet isn't busy trying to kill me. When I look out further, to the horizon, I spy my target.

"There!" I say, pointing at the dark pillar rising on the horizon.

It looks like a sword thrusting towards the sky. Or a finger. Yeah, a finger, one telling all the gods and the entire universe where to shove it. That fits better. The small group looks back then follows where I'm pointing.

"The ship?" Isla asks.

"Yes," I say.

Say it like you mean it. Like you have a clue what you're doing. It works. The group murmurs, nods, then shifts the direction of their steps towards the ship. Only Morgana hangs to the back and watches me with a knowing smile on her face.

I do not understand that woman at all. Having a destination invigorates me, and I pull on some deep reserves. I rush past the group and take the lead. I'm moving fast. Well, faster than we were, and the rest of them struggle to keep up.

Every time we hit the bottom side of a dune, the ship is blocked from sight. It's only when we crest the next that I can course correct, and somehow, each time we do, we're off again. I'm not sure how we keep managing to not walk a straight line, but we're doing it like champions.

There's nothing I can do about it except keep walking. After repeating this a dozen times, I stop and wipe the sweat from my brow. Every part of my body hurts. Some parts ache, some parts throb, and then there's the pulse-matching pounding in my head.

Squinting my eyes and trying to see past the pain, I study the way ahead and try to figure out why the hell we can't walk straight. I got nothing. When my eyes follow the horizon line, something tugs at my attention.

"Morgana," I say. "Come here."

Morgana climbs back up the dune to stand next to me. I point towards a blob that seems closer than the ship.

"Right," Morgana says. "That's the oasis."

I rub my temples, then roll my head trying to find some relief. "Okay, let's go that way. We're heading for an Oasis. Remember the one we got water and wood from when we stayed at the ship?"

Murmurs of assent come from the group. I don't wait for more. Using the momentum of going downhill, I race past them, and it helps me make it halfway up the next dune before I'm struggling again. Problem with a desert planet is that the sand is loose. It's not always, but a lot of times the top layer is deep, and you sink in. Sometimes deep means, 'up to your knees.'

This son-of-a-bitch dune is one of those. Every step is a fight. I heard someone came up with an idea for 'sand-shoes' but they've never caught on because they take a specific wood that is in short supply. Welcome to Tajss. Everything is in short supply.

All of us help each other until we're at the summit of the dune. I'm fighting for the last few steps when my back foot sticks, and I fall forward. I put my hands out and barely keep myself from face-planting. As I'm pushing myself back upright, I feel them again.

Vibrations. Stronger. Much, much stronger.

My heart races as adrenaline pumps into my body. I leap up and forwards, mounting the dune and turning around. The glow of engines is impossible to miss. Three machines are racing straight for us.

"RUN!" I scream, pointing at the oasis.

Every nerve in my body wants to do that too, but I force myself to stay. I grab Isla's hand and pull her over the peak then push her to keep moving while I help Eloise and the rest of them. I don't move until they're all over the top.

When I turn and run, I'm not far behind the group, which is spreading out. Clothes fluttering, arms and legs flailing, we race up and down the rolling dunes.

To what?

The oasis doesn't offer any safety. There's no protective force-field dome to protect us. Only idiots wouldn't be able to find us hiding in the trees. I force that voice of logic to shut up. It's better than waiting here for them to capture us.

The oasis is right there. The first of our group runs into its cover. I'm at the back of the group, but the sound of those rumbling engines is so close, the vibrations are shaking in my chest. When Morgana looks over her shoulder, her eyes and mouth stretch wide, but I can't hear what she screams.

Something slams into my back and I hit the ground. Sand fills my mouth, eyes, and nose. The weight on my back feels like a ton. Terrified, I struggle, desperate to get up, to breathe free air.

I get my head up, gasping air while spitting out sand. I dig my hands into the sand, crawling forward. The weight lifts off my back and I scramble ahead on my belly.

When I roll over I'm looking up at one of the massive, four-armed, blue-skinned Invaders. There's an evil grin on his face, but his yellowish eyes stare, unblinking. He takes a step forward.

Fear and rage vie for control of my tired brain. Rage wins.

I leap off the ground, fingers curled into claws. Slamming into his chest, I claw at his vulnerable eyes.

He laughs but it only serves to fuel the rage. I scratch, claw, and bite. Kick, hit, anything to hurt him.

He grabs the back of my shirt and jerks me off of him. Flailing my arms and legs, I twist my head trying to bite his arm. He shakes me. Hard. My head bangs around, and for a moment all I see is stars, but I keep fighting. My vision clears, and my heart stops when it does.

A dozen Invaders have fanned out to either side of my captor. It's over. We're done.

6

KHABRI

THE TWINS, PACHUA AND TYPHON, LEAD THE WAY AS WE RUN across the desert. We must reach the City. It's our best chance to rally an offensive against the Invaders. If we can't drive them back, then I'll be forced to activate the Devastation Protocols.

Even in my thoughts I shy away from that. Once is enough. Now, without the guidance and vision of The Eye, I don't know that we would recover. Tajss would, though. That is more important.

We run in silence. Each of us alone with our thoughts, no matter the group around us. I feel my brethren's pain. It's a low hum thrumming beneath my thoughts. I understand it, for all of these males have lost everything they know.

They've sworn their loyalty to the Order, to the vision of The Eye, but they don't live every day with that higher purpose as I do. They are soldiers, told what they need to know. The bigger picture, long-term strategy, all is beyond their training and experience.

We run for the City but take a wide, arcing path towards our destination. Mageir moves to run beside me. It's obvious he has something to say, so I nod my assent.

"Sir," he says. "Will they follow us?"

"Yes," I say. "I am sure of that."

He nods, frowning. The troubled look on his face makes it obvious he has more to say. I wait, letting him work it out.

"Why did we run, sir?" he asks the real question at last.

"And if we hadn't?"

"We'd have killed them!" he growls.

"Would we?"

The rest of the group has moved in closer. They're all listening. This is the question on all of their minds. They are warriors, retreating from a fight goes against every instinct they have.

"Yes, *sir!*" he replies, emphasizing the sir.

"How many are there with us?"

"Sir?" he asks, looking around at our small group.

"How many survivors, soldier?"

He looks around, doing a count. His scales are tinted with anger, but I see confusion on his face.

"Ten, counting you, sir," he says at last.

"Ten," I agree. "Tell me, Mageir, how many soldiers were in the compound during the attack?"

"Twenty-three patrols at least," he answers.

"Twenty-three patrols, so forty-six warriors."

"Yes sir," he says, still not getting it.

"What would have happened had we stayed and fought?" I change directions.

"We'd have destroyed them all," Vae responds, to which most of the group mutters their agreement.

"The ten of us? Five patrols out of twenty-three?" I ask.

"Yes, sir!" five of the males answer in unison.

"We'd have died," Pachua and Typhon says in unison. "All of us."

Silence surrounds us as we continue running blindly into the night. I don't say any more, let them work it out in their own heads. They'll come to terms, sooner or later.

The group spreads out again. The sky is brightening, but no one complains of exhaustion. Still, we're without supplies and we need water as well as rest. I shift our direction towards an oasis that won't be far out of our way.

Ahead, Pachua and Typhon drop to their bellies on the peak of a dune. As one, the group stops. I crouch and move up to join them. Pachua points a finger and I follow it.

Invader vehicles race across the desert towards the same oasis I was leading us towards. We'll have to avoid it, but I'm sure we can make the City without water. I rise and turn to instruct the group when suddenly it feels as if there is a weight on my back making it too hard to breathe.

I whirl around and look again. The machines have come to a stop. The Invaders run across the desert, chasing... no.

I spread my wings and leap into motion. I hit the sand running, pulling the lochaber off of my back.

I lose sight of them at the bottom of the dune, but nothing can slow me down. She's there. She's in trouble. I will myself to run faster. My muscles are burning, but the power of the dragon's raging fire swirls through my veins.

Every step I take, I leap ahead. Faster!

Dimly I hear the rest of the group rushing to catch me, but there's no time. I must save her. Cresting the final dune, I see her form. An Invader has her. I can't make out her face in the early dawn light. But it's her.

A dozen Invaders form a semi-circle to either side of the one holding her and are marching towards the oasis. There must be more humans hiding in there.

My legs and arms pumping, a fresh burst of energy thrills through my muscles. I whirl the lochaber, and it screams a challenge as it slices the air, hungry for Invader flesh. A hot breeze blows from behind and I leap. I snap my wings wide, angle them to catch the wind, gliding faster than I can run.

She fights the Invader. She's like a wild animal, captured but not beaten. My chest swells with so much pride and love, it hurts. My dragon howls, and I can't contain its voice.

"TO ME!" I scream in a full-throated roar.

The Invader holding my mate whirls around. She flops violently in his grip. Red hazes my vision that he handles her in such a reckless manner. He will pay.

I slam to the ground a tail's length before him. There is no hesitation, no pause—I attack. He throws my mate to one side, and two clubs and a blade whirl in a now-familiar pattern. I jab, trying to thrust my way past his defense.

The two clubs slam against my lochaber. Numbing vibrations race up my arms. I shift my hands to keep my grip at the same time I swing my tail low. He leaps up and over.

I jerk the lochaber's blade back then stab forward. He blocks with the sword because the clubs are out of position, but I surprise him. I tilt my body down and drive the top of my head into his face. My horns gouge flesh as the soft bones of his nose and jaw smash.

His blood spews, blocking my vision in one eye, but he's stumbling back dropping his weapons. I finish him with the lochaber.

The rest of my brethren arrive and engage the others. Wiping furiously at my eyes, I race to my mate, skidding to a stop on my knees next to her.

My hands tremble as I reach towards her. The dragon's rumbling assures me she is the one. The one I've sought so long. The emptiness aching in my soul hungers, ready to welcome her. She's lying limp on the ground but emits a low groan. One hand rises to her forehead.

She is so perfect. It hurts to look at her. My stomach knots and I can't catch my breath. It's as if I've taken a hit to the solar plexus. My fingers are inches from her beautiful, soft skin, but I can't force them closer. I don't dare touch her, lest she disappear in a puff of smoke, for surely, she is a dream.

She is an angel from the stars. The embodiment of Tajss herself given form as an exotic, strangely erotic alien. Her hair covers most of her face, so it's hard to decipher its color in the dim light, but her hair appears to be a deep rich brown.

Swallowing hard, I force my hand to move, pushing past my frozen state, but before I touch her, she stirs, and I stop again. Her hand touching her head pushes aside her hair. Bright, intelligent eyes flash hotly, and then in an instant she rolls over.

"Ah!" she cries out, scrabbling away.

"It is okay," I say. "We have saved you."

She shakes her head from side to side, but she stops retreating. I hold myself still as stone, letting her realize she is safe. It will only take a moment, I'm sure. She was assaulted, handled roughly, so she is scared, and I do not blame her. She does not have to worry now though. I will not allow any male to touch her in such a way again.

"Who..." she says, stopping to wipe a trickle of blood from her forehead. "are you?"

She has a round face. More round than most of the human females I've seen, it is an almost perfect oval. Her nose is tiny, perfect on her, though it is slightly humped as if it has been broken before. I commit every stunning line to memory.

"I am Khabri," I say. "I've been looking for you."

"Us?" she asks, looking around.

When her brow furrows her delicate eyebrows pinch together and a tiny wrinkle forms between them. Her lips are full and plush, trembling. I desperately want to kiss them.

"Not us," I correct her gently. "You."

"Me?" she shakes her head and shifts to a full sitting position.

The last of the Invaders meets his end with a raucous scream and silence falls. Pachua and Typhon walk over, and my mate moves further back, staring at them. I hold up my hand, stopping their approach.

"Are there more humans?" I ask. She bites her lip, looking from one member of the Order to the next. Fear and uncertainty are written plainly across her face. She nods at last. I deliberately soften my voice to say, "How many?"

"I'm not telling you," she says. "Leave us alone."

She confuses me. Why would I leave her alone? Does she not feel the connection throbbing between us? As I look at her, the world keeps clicking further into place, as if everything in my entire life has been nothing but a prelude leading me to this moment. To her.

I don't understand, but I don't want to force her into anything either. Swallowing my hurt and confusion, I hold my hands up, palms facing her.

"It is dangerous," I say. "There are more of them. We will protect you."

My brethren are stomping through the oasis looking for the others. Typhon and Pachua are close by, but the others are looking for the humans. We shouldn't stay here for long, there may well be more Invaders not far away.

There is a commotion inside the trees, and then a human male runs out. He is screaming, almost as if he himself is a female. I stare in amazement. Why he is acting like this?

"No! Stay away! No! No! No!" he screams, and now he's running in a circle while Nidhus, Mageir, and Iriden attempt to corral and calm him. They're not helping the situation. I rise up and look at Pachua and Typhon.

"Stop that," I order.

They salute and go to intervene. I return my attention to my mate. I don't understand her any more than I understand that male acting as he is.

"I have been looking for you," I start again. "For a very long time. I've felt your presence—here." I hold my hand over my chest.

She arches one eyebrow then climbs to her feet.

"You're kidding," she says.

"I would never joke about this," I say. "You are my treasure. I've looked for you everywhere, or so I thought. I am grateful to finally find you."

She snorts, covering her mouth with the back of her hand. This must be a human custom. I am not aware of its import or meaning, though. Her eyes glisten with moisture. "Tears," they call this "tears" in her kind. I've studied all the data we had on her race. It doesn't clarify what is happening because, unfortunately, our research shows they can shed them for both joy and sadness.

It is a wasteful exercise, but then humans aren't genetically predisposed to life on Tajss. She will need epis so her body can adjust. It will also improve her ability to bear our children.

"We don't need *your* help," a human male yells, jerking my attention away from her.

My blood warms. All I want is to talk to my mate. Why, in the name of Tajss, do there have to be so many distractions? Her attention is drawn to the disagreement, which angers me more. I'll have to deal with this first.

"One moment, my treasure," I say, turning away.

"I'm not your treasure," she says, but I ignore that.

A human male is glaring at Vae and Mageir. His hands are balled into fists, his face is flushed red, and he's shaking. The tension in the air is so thick it's become hard to breathe. I find my center, pulling calm over myself. Standing straighter, holding my head high, and squaring my shoulders as I assume the manner of a Council Member.

"What is happening?" I ask, pointedly ignoring the human male.

"This male and the others," Vae says, motioning towards the gathered humans, "are declining our assistance."

"We don't need any filthy *lizards* to help us," the male says.

"Petras, seriously," my treasure says, inserting herself into the conversation.

The one she calls Petras shoots a hateful glare in her direction. Rage consumes my thoughts like an erupting fire, and I step towards him before I can slam in control. Even so, my thoughts are tinged with red and the pulsing desire to harm him for daring to look at her in such a way.

"Petras," I say, and it comes out like a curse. "Your people need our help. We will get you to the City and your own kind."

"I already said we don't need your help," he snaps. "Are you deaf as well as dumb?"

Vae tightens his grip on his lochaber and Iriden growls. Petras has enough sense to take a step back from them, but he's not going to back down. I look the humans over. They're dirty and exhausted. Their clothes are torn, and most of them are weaving on their feet, barely able to remain standing. The idea they will make it on their own is laughable.

"Invaders?" I ask.

"Your friends?" Petras asks.

"We are also running from them," I admit. "Let us help you."

"We. Don't. Need. You," he bites off each word.

"Then tell me," I say. "How will you reach the City on your own? Tajss has many more dangers than Invaders. Not to mention, they've found you once."

"I'm taking their machines." He points to their vehicles.

"That is not a good idea," I say.

57

My treasure moves closer and my hearts beat faster. Blood races to my brain making me light-headed. She's approaching. The connection between us is throbbing with pent up energy. She feels it too!

My stomach tightens as if I've been struck when she moves to stand next to Petras instead of me. I blink rapidly as my thoughts race. What is she doing? Why? And the softest of whispers, am I wrong?

When she touches his shoulder, I'm blinded by my own rage. My hand tightens on my lochaber. One step, one thrust, and I will end him.

"Petras," she says. "We need them."

"No, we don't," he says, turning to face her.

The other humans huddle closer around the two of them. Several of them speak, softly, but still speaking out in favor of letting us help them. Some hang back and say nothing, while others voice their agreement with Petras.

My treasure looks at me, and my chest swells. My tail stiffens and I feel like I'm taller, bigger. She is all.

"Why can't we use their vehicles?" she asks.

"They are able to track them," I explain. "If they go off an expected path, they will most likely send fliers and bomb them."

"See," she says to Petras. "He's trying to help."

"You're turning into one of *them,*" he spits the last word.

"Shit Petras, give it up," she says, clutching the hair on the top of her head, leaning back, and looking at the sky. "Gershom is dead. The Humans First Movement is dead. Earth isn't going to rescue us, and we are screwed. Our home is burning! We've lost everything, again. How many are dead back there? All I'm saying is, letting them help us is better than dying out here on our own."

"Fine, but I don't trust them," he says, turning and stomping to the back of the assembled humans.

I gaze at her with open admiration. She handled the situation as a leader. If she were a member of the Order, I'd groom her towards being a Councilor one day. Intelligent, practical, and obviously willing to do whatever it takes.

"Gather what belongings you have," I order. "We must keep moving. This will not go unanswered by the Invaders."

"Why are they doing this?" a tiny human female asks. She's so small she might be a child, but she has the body of a grown woman.

"They are taking over Tajss," I say. Whispers race through the humans in a soft murmur of gasps and expressions of disbelief or fear. "We must reach the City and do whatever it takes to stop them."

My treasure walks to me. My breath catches in my throat. My scales tingle, aching for the briefest of her touches.

"You're serious?" she whispers.

"I am," I say.

"You're… Order?" she asks.

A lump forms in my throat making it hard to answer. Am I Order? Or is the Order destroyed? Even if it is, our mission carries on. Tajss must be saved so, no matter what, I am still Order.

"Yes," I answer.

"Is this all of you?" she asks, looking at the others over her shoulder.

"Yes," I answer.

"We're going to need a bigger army."

7

CALISTA

"AND THEN HE STORMED OUT THE DOOR," I SAY.

"You're kidding?" Jolie asks.

"No," I say, shaking my head. "I don't get it. Why can't he let this go? It almost cost us everything. How can he possibly think it's a good idea?"

Jolie frowns as she grabs another piece of clothing and dunks it into the tub of cold water. She works the cloth between her hands, rubbing it against itself before pushing it down and working it across the stones at the bottom.

"Do you think he's scared?" she asks.

"Scared? Of what?" I ask.

"I don't know," she shakes her head. "A full invasion? Losing control?"

"It's not like him," I say. "I don't understand what's happening. He's acting different."

"I get it," she says. "It's been really tough lately. The lockdown didn't do anyone any favors."

"Right?" I sigh taking the wet shirt from her and then laying it out on the hot rocks to dry. "I'm ready for normal." Jolie laughs. "What?"

"How many years did you think it would take before we started thinking of life on Tajss as 'normal'?" she asks.

Frowning, I think about it. "Never?"

"Exactly!" she exclaims.

"Mommy! Mommy! Mommy!" Rverre is yelling as she runs up to us.

She skids to a stop in front of Jolie as I scan the area for Illadon. He won't be far. They're inseparable.

"What?" Jolie asks.

Rverre holds up a tiny, sparkling rock. "Look!"

"Wow," Jolie says, examining the rock closely. "That's really pretty."

"I know, I found it," she says. "I'm going to make it into a necklace."

Illadon appears on top of a large pile of rubble next to one of the broken buildings across the square. Other people are moving around the fountain, the one source of water in the City, on their way to their jobs or hanging out. This has become a central gathering point for everyone who lives here. Illadon is jumping up and down as if he's trying to tamp down the rocks.

"What is he doing?" I mutter.

"He thinks he can jump up to the second story," Rverre says. "I told him it was stupid, but he didn't want to listen to me."

"Please tell him that if he doesn't quit, he's going to be in big trouble," I say.

"Okay!" she exclaims and runs off in a puff of dust and scrabbling of clawed toes on concrete.

"Slow down!" Jolie yells at her retreating daughter, but it's a perfunctory order that carries no weight and has the same effect on Rverre—nothing.

"He's too much like his father," I grouse. "Stubborn and intent on doing something stupid."

"I don't think Ladon intends to do something stupid," Jolie says. "He's worried."

"Why?" I ask, snapping the wet shirt like a whip. "We haven't seen the Invaders in months. We haven't even had any Zzlo sightings for a long time. The bivo taming project is progressing, the Tribe has vegetables growing, and the miners are delivering raw material. We'll be able to fully repair buildings soon.

Our life is good! Why isn't it good enough for him? What is there to worry about?"

"I don't know," Jolie says. "But I feel something too. Amara says Malcolm has been even more morose than usual. It's why she didn't bring him out to do laundry with us."

"I don't want to be mean," I say. "But Malcolm is odd."

"Yeah," Jolie says. "But he's also always right. Last time Olivia came to the City, she was saying that Zoe does that thing too, where she knows things there's no way she could know."

"I guess we're the lucky ones," I say. "Our kids are just... kids."

Half-alien kids, sure, with scales, tails, and nubby horns, but kids.

"True," Jolie agrees.

"It doesn't change the facts either," I say, returning to my tirade which feels unfinished. I love Ladon with all that I am. The only thing that competes in my heart with him is Illadon, but he's really irritating me. "Life is good! Look at all we've managed to do in such a short time!"

"Hey, I don't disagree our lives are good," Jolie says. "I'm playing devil's advocate for you."

"I know, sorry," I say, realizing I'm getting harsh with her. She's my best friend, and she is trying to help. The least I can do is not be a bitch.

"So he really wanted you to agree to go away with him?" she asks.

"Yeah," I say. "Leave it all. You, the City, all of it."

I stretch a wet pair of pants out on the rack.

"That's it," Jolie says, rising from her knees and stretching her back. "I think it's about time for the Council meeting. These should be dry when we get back."

"Sounds good," I agree. Turning around I look at where the kids are playing. "Think they'll be okay?"

Jolie shields her eyes with a hand and frowns. "Yeah."

"Illadon! I'll be back after the meetings. Be good!"

Illadon waves from the top of the pile. Rverre climbs up from behind to stand next to him.

"I'll make sure!" she yells.

Jolie snorts. "That helps."

"They've been fine for the past three hours while we worked, I'm sure they'll be okay. They always are," I say.

As we turn to walk toward the Council meeting, I spy Lana and call out to her.

"Yeah?" she asks, a woven basket on her hip and her boy Aeros toddling along beside her.

"Can you keep an eye on the kids?" I ask.

"Sure," she says. "Where are they?"

I point to where their playing.

"Illadon?" Aeros asks, a smile playing across his tiny, cherubic face.

"Yes," I smile. "You want to play with him?"

"Can I?" he asks Lana.

"Yes, darling," Lana agrees.

"Okay, Aeros," I say, kneeling to be eye level with him. "You make sure he doesn't get in trouble, okay? Can you do that for me?"

His face is very serious. He frowns deeply as he nods. "Yes, I make sure."

"Good," I say, tousling his hair. "Thank you, Lana."

"Of course," she says. "How's things looking?"

"Good," I lie, cutting off Jolie before she can speak. "Real good."

"It's a lot easier now that the lockdown is lifted," Lana says.

"Isn't it? Okay, we have to go," I say, and Lana nods.

We make our way to the building where the Council meetings are held before Jolie speaks.

"Why'd you lie to her?" she asks.

"Because she'll worry," I say. "What good does that do her or anyone?"

Jolie frowns, but her nod shows understanding if not agreement. Climbing the stairs to the Council Chamber my heart is racing and it's not from the exercise. A crushing pressure weighs down, sucking the life and joy out of everything.

"Are you okay?" Jolie asks when we're about halfway there.

"No," I admit, looking down and wiping the stinging tears away.

She places her hand on the small of my back as we continue climbing. I blink several times to clear my eyes, take a few deep breaths, then nod that I'm okay. She smiles and we keep climbing.

"Above all else, he loves you," Jolie says.

"And I love him," I say. "This wouldn't hurt so damn bad if I didn't. Maybe then I could let it go or let him be, but he's changing in front of me and I don't know what to do. Ladon's always been intense, driven, but this is… different. It's more."

"Maybe Rosalind will help," Jolie offers. "He needs somewhere to focus his energy."

"Let's hope so," I say. We've reached the end of the last stairway and stand before the doors to the receiving chamber outside the conference room. I wipe sweat from my brow. "Remind me why we thought it was a good idea to have the conference room up this many flights of stairs?"

"I always figured it was to reduce the number of complaints," Jolie says.

"Huh?"

"It's too many stairs to climb for a minor bitch. You have to have something pretty serious on your mind to make it all the way up," she says with a wide grin.

I laugh and shake my head. As she reaches for the door, I grab her, pulling her into a tight embrace.

"Thank you," I whisper into her neck and hair.

She returns the embrace and we hold each other for a moment, then straighten and walk across the hall to the Council Chamber.

Amara and Shidan sit on the left, Sverre and Ladon are seated on the right. Astarot is pacing the room in circles while Rosalind and Visidion sit side-by-side at the head of the long, thick table. Everyone looks as we walk in, but my attention is on Ladon.

The coloring at the edges of his scales is a hue of red that I know too well, especially lately. He's already angry. If that's not enough, it's clear in his posture, the stiffness in his tail, the look in his eyes. It all screams, "Rage!"

"I believe we're all here now," Rosalind says, then she raps the table with her knuckles, calling the meeting to order.

I split from Jolie and take my seat next to Ladon while she sits next to Sverre. Ladon's eyes study me as I walk closer and sit down. He places his hand over mine and squeezes, but it's the only acknowledgement he gives me.

My stomach ties into knots. Is this what we've become? How can he be so cold? Where is the warmth of his smile?

"I want to keep this short today," Rosalind says. "Addison

says we have had no new cases of the virus and that the vaccine she developed is working."

"Good," Astarot says, moving to take a stool at the table.

"I am going to consider that problem handled," Rosalind continues. "There is no other old business before the Council. Is there new business to be conducted?"

Ladon looks at me and the conflict is written clearly across his face. Fire burns in his eyes, but we're connected. I know what he's thinking and understand him in a way I can't with any other person. A barely perceptible nod, then he rises.

"Yes," he says, his cool hand still resting on mine.

"We are now immune to the virus from the bunker," he says. "I now propose that we go there and find a way to activate the missiles. The Invaders are still in our skies. It is time that we handle this matter permanently. We must protect ourselves."

"They're gone," I interject.

"They are not," he says, staring straight ahead.

Cold crawls across my skin. He's not looking at me. Is he that angry? Or is it because he can't? He can't look at me when he's fighting with me?

"What evidence do you bring that they are not?" Rosalind asks. "It seemed they came for the meteorite glass."

"That would be an assumption," Sverre says.

"Yes," Rosalind nods. "One we have been successfully operating with for a long time."

"Why provoke an act of war?" Visidion asks. "We have peace. We are growing. This is no time for conflict."

"If we don't act first, they will!" Ladon yells, squeezing my hand so tight it hurts and slamming his other fist down on the table.

Rosalind's eyes narrow and she tightens her jaw, but she doesn't say anything.

"Ladon, there is no cause for this," I say.

He jerks his hand off mine and turns to me.

"I will not sit by and let harm come to you or Illadon," he growls. "No matter if you try to stand in my way."

Shock like I've been dunked in ice water hits me. I'm rocked back by his vehemence and accusation. Tears blur my vision. I open my mouth to protest, but no words come.

"Ladon," Rosalind says. She doesn't raise her voice, but the command is in it all the same. Ladon slowly turns to face her. "Sit down."

He stands defiant, shaking. The tension in the room rises. No one moves. No one breathes. Ladon drops to his stool, bowing his head, hands clenched tight on the table in front of him.

"None of you believe this," he says, his voice quiet. "I am right."

I bow my head and wipe at my tears. This doesn't feel real.

"I'm open to discussion," Rosalind says.

"There have been raids by these Invaders after the meteor showers stopped," Astarot says.

"This is true," Sverre chimes in.

"I can't say I'm ready to take action that would start a war," Amara says. "But you yourself used to say the best way to stop a war is to be prepared before one starts."

Rosalind purses her lips and nods agreement that she did say that.

"It's not enough to be prepared," Ladon says. "We are a target. They want more, they want Tajss."

Rosalind looks at Visidion who shrugs then nods. Rosalind touches his arm. Something passes between the two of them as they look at each other.

"When Rosalind and I were on the planet Krik," Visidion says, "we learned many things, most of which we've shared with you all here."

He rises to his feet, looking at his audience. Pinpricks race along my limbs, knowing that something is happening.

"Before the Devastation there was a galactic war," Visidion continues. "Twelve planets, each against the other in a web of ever-shifting politics and alliances."

"Sure," Amara says. "But why? What were they fighting over?"

"Tajss," Visidion says. It hits us like a bomb going off.

"Why?" I ask.

"Epis," Rosalind says. "The control of epis."

No one speaks as a lot of pieces fall into place. It's like putting together a puzzle when you get to those key pieces that make the whole thing make sense.

"You think that it's starting again," I exhale.

"We told you about Arcan, the Zmaj we met on Krik who took over as King of the planet," Rosalind says.

"His goal was to continue hiding the fact that life survived on Tajss," Visidion finishes. "It seems that goal has failed."

"Then if they're not here for the glass," I say.

"That's why they're always attacking the Tribe more than here?" Sverre asks.

"It could be," Rosalind says. "It would make sense. They have the direct source of epis open and being farmed."

"They won't stop," Ladon says. "They will see Tajss burn, again, rather than not control it. They raped the planet before the Devastation. We must act now, with finality."

"We don't know any of this!" I exclaim. "You can't go to war when you don't know there's something to fight about."

"*I* know," Ladon growls, and I jerk back in shock. "I must do this. We *must.*"

Hurt and surprise wrestle in my head. I'm stunned. I can' t respond because my mouth won't work. I don't know what to do or say. He's never, in our seven years together, acted so roughly with me. He's never spoken to me in a tone like that, not even when he was lost to his bijass because of the virus.

His face softens and he reaches towards me, but I pull back. My eyes fill, and it's all I can do to keep the tears from falling. I don't want to cry here in front of everyone.

"Ladon," Rosalind says. He looks away from me to her. "We understand the stakes. I also understand Calista's viewpoint and she's not wrong. We don't want to start a fight we can't finish."

"There are dozens of warriors frozen in that bunker," he says. "We'll wake them up. That will swell our ranks. We'll have an army!"

"We don't know why those males are there," Sverre says.

"They could be frozen for a reason," Astarot says. "It would not be wise to try to awaken them before we understand."

"There is no time!" Ladon slams his fist. The loud crack echoes in the silence that follows it. "They will come. I know it. I will not sit idle while my family is in danger. Either we strike first, or we move to a safer location, one they don't know about."

"Do you have one?" Visidion asks.

Ladon snaps his mouth shut, looks at me, then stares at the table. It isn't very long, but it feels like it is. He shakes his head negative, but I know in my bones he's lying. He knows something that he isn't sharing. No one calls him on it, so I keep my mouth shut.

"The missiles are our best hope," Ladon insists. "I am going. One way or another."

"I don't want you going back there," I say.

It slips out. I'm not speaking as a Council Member. I'm not thinking of the greater good or the future of humans and Zmaj. I'm speaking as a wife, a mother, a woman desperately in love with her mate. Ladon turns back to me, and there is no anger in his face, but only sadness.

"I must," he says, speaking softly.

"I forbid it!" I yell. "You're not going back there. It almost killed you last time and I won't have it!"

"Calis—" Jolie says rising from her seat.

"I *will* do what *must* be done," Ladon says cutting off Jolie and pulling himself up to his full height so that he towers over me.

I'd started out of my seat, but I drop onto my ass so hard it hurts my tailbone. His wings are partway open and his tail is raised between them, the tip vibrating behind his head. Rage. He's experiencing rage. At me?

"Who will go with you?" Rosalind asks.

I see the look on her face, empathy and sympathy. She's attempting to defuse the situation, but there's no going back. He's crossing bridges that shouldn't be touched.

"I will attend him," Sverre says.

"I'll go," Astarot says.

"Fine, let's go," Ladon says.

He pauses when our eyes meet. The fire of his anger burns in them, but beneath the fire, I imagine I see something more. Begging. Begging for forgiveness, for understanding, but I don't. My chest constricts and I can't get a good breath. My heart hurts so badly I want to curl up and cry.

He waits as my heart struggles to beat, once, twice, on to four times, but I don't have whatever it is he wants. I can't forgive him. This is too much. He's going too far, and he isn't talking to me about why. He's shutting me out.

He blinks, closes his wings, then strides past me without a word or touch. I watch the door close behind him and the other two males. It shuts with a heavy finality, and it shatters my heart.

8

ANNA

Sophia stumbles forward and barely manages to stop herself from falling. Aurora, Emma, and Liam gather around her and offer their support, not that they're in any better shape. We're all hurting, bad. The suns came up hours ago, but we're still stumbling across the desert.

We need a break, except we can't take one. Every time I think about stopping, images of our fallen comrades, left behind at the settlement, float across my thoughts. I keep digging deeper and somehow finding the strength to carry on.

The crazy Zmaj continues to call me his treasure. I know damn well what that means, and he's got another think coming, thank you very much. Except right now I'm too tired to argue. He's never far away, not too close, but still right there out of the corner of my eye.

I feel his eyes on the back of my neck. He looks at me with an intensity that heats my skin and makes warmth coil in my belly. Which is stupid. I'm not dating a Zmaj. Uh-uh, no way. If nothing else I've heard what the girls say about them and their monster dongs. Thanks, but no thanks. I don't need any monster-porn dong.

"We need to rest," Petras says, stumbling to a stop.

"Where?" I ask, wiping sweat from my brow for the umpteen millionth time.

It's official. I'm wiped, I don't even have the energy to argue with Petras, and that's one of my favorite pastimes. He's such a douche-nozzle moron. Petras turns in a circle as if he might magically find shelter.

"Anywhere," he says, throwing his hands up.

"There's lots of shade up your ass," I snap.

"Who in the hell put you in charge?" he yells with a surprising burst of energy.

"When it became clear I'm smart enough to know that if we stop here, we'll bake to death because there's no shelter," I tell him.

No one speaks, but everyone resumes walking so my point is made.

"How much farther can it be?" I ask.

"About a half day, my treasure," the creeper Zmaj says helpfully.

"I'm not your treasure," I say wearily.

Half a day. Shit. Good news, we're almost there. Bad news, I can't feel my feet. Or my legs. Or my butt, come to think of it. Do I still have an ass? I hope so. I've always liked my ass. Nice, curvy, fills out a pair of pants well.

"You are," he insists, cutting into my disarray of thoughts.

"What's your name?" I ask. I don't look at him only because it's too much effort to turn my head.

"I am Khabri," he says.

"Well, Khabri," I say. "I don't know you, and I'm sure as hell not looking for love. So let's get this cleared up. I'm not your treasure, your mate, or hell, even your friend, at least not yet. I don't know you, get it?"

"You will," he says with a smugness that pisses me off.

I'm opening my mouth to tell him just how much he is pissing me off when his overly large hand clamps down over my lips. Instantly I'm in fight mode. I bite down, but he moves his hand out then back on, holding my mouth shut. I kick him as hard as I can in the shin. I'm happy he grunts, but he doesn't let go.

"Quiet," he hisses.

The Zmaj have formed a circle around us, facing out. I nod understanding, seeing that he's not being rape-y or something. He moves his hand, and moving in slow motion he kneels, placing a hand flat on the sands and closing his eyes.

I look at the others, trying to comprehend what he's doing and why they're all acting on edge. The ground vibrates under my feet, and the sand slides down the dune we came down a moment ago.

"Run," Khabri says, rising and pointing behind us. "We'll hold its attention. Run to the City, take the humans." I'm staring wide-eyed, not comprehending in my exhaustion. "Run!"

When he yells, I snap to and turn to the others. I motion with my hands, and they stumble into motion. It's far from what I would call a run, a lumbering slow shamble describes it better, but we're moving.

As I watch over my shoulder, the Zmaj fan out into a semi-circle and draw their lochabers.

Suddenly the ground in front of them explodes. Dirt and sand fly high into the air, obscuring my vision. I can't see the Zmaj at all. Emerging from the cloud of filth is a thing of nightmares.

"Zemlja!" someone screams, and then it's on.

Full panic grips all my fellow humans, and they're running while screaming. I try to run, but something hits me in the back of the head. Stars dancing across my sight, I'm thrown forward.

I stumble several steps before I lose it and fall to my hands and knees.

I put my hand to the back of my head and touch something wet and sticky. Blood stains my fingers trembling in front of my face. My stomach clenches tight, and for a moment, I'm sure I'm going to throw up. There's nothing in my stomach to lose, which I'm thankful about.

"Hurry up!" Liam yells, grabbing my right arm. Elijah is grabbing my left arm, and they're dragging me with them.

I scramble until my feet are under me and I'm running with the group. One glance back, and I realize I've really got to quit. It's not good back there. I don't want to know.

The Zmaj are fighting the monster worm. It's a ginormous dick with a gaping maw filled with thousands of teeth. It's like a space slug from *Empire Strikes Back* except bigger and more teeth, more cock like.

Damn, how hard did I get hit in the head? I'm insane. Running for my life and coming up with comparisons of a zemlja and a space slug-slash-dick? Get it together, girl!

The zemlja screeches, and then the three of us are flying through the air. The ground was nicely under my feet, as it should be, then next step, it's not. I'm flailing like an idiot trying to run on air, which is not working.

I'm screaming as I fly forward. The ground races up towards me. This is going to hurt. A dozen possible idea flit through my head, ways I might get out of this, but they're all stupid or impossible. I close my eyes to brace for the impact that's going to come any second. I'm on this ride until the end.

The ground is every bit as hard as I expect it to be. I tuck my head and slam down shoulder first, trying to roll and take out the brunt of the hit. It helps, I think, but the wind is knocked out of me, and everything hurts.

Shakily, I climb to my feet. Liam and Elijah lie in heaps to either side, but Liam is moving, so I run to Elijah. He's moving when I reach him, groaning.

"Get up!" I yell, grabbing his arm and pulling.

He groans but gets up. The hairs on the back of my neck stand on end as cold races down my spine.

"NO!" Khabri yells from some distance behind me.

I don't want to turn around. I know it's bad. Every fiber of my being is screaming don't look, run, but don't look.

I look.

My stomach drops, leaving me shaking as I will myself to run, but there's no way. The almighty evil dick of Tajss itself is about to fuck me, and there's no escaping it. I can't even scream. I try, but a pathetic whimpering sound comes out.

I'm struck from the side, and then rolling across the hard-packed sand. Over and over, sand getting in my eyes, mouth, and nose but still we're rolling. I bounce up into the air, slam down, and still rolling.

When I come to a stop, it takes a second to realize that Liam has his arms and legs wrapped around me. I struggle to a sitting position looking back.

"Elijah!" I scream.

He's running, zigzagging, but there's no hope. The zemlja keeps rising from under the ground, towering over the desert dozens of feet high. It bends impossibly far, mouth opening wide, then it crashes down, burrowing back under the ground—taking Elijah with it.

"NO!" I scream, reaching my hand towards where he was.

Tears stream down my face, but I don't care. No one deserves to die like that. I fight my way free of Liam and stumble towards the hole the damn worm left behind. I don't have a plan, but somehow, I have to save him.

The ground rumbles again, and I come to my senses enough to realize how incredibly stupid what I'm doing is. Khabri appears beside me, scoops me up in one arm, and runs. I see the other Zmaj are not far behind, and they're grabbing up the other humans, including Liam.

The dirt and sand is bouncing, which apparently means the zemlja is still hunting. I wrap my arms around Khabri's neck and stare behind him.

The armor of numb is cracking, and emotions I don't want to deal with are slipping through. I sob and shudder as I try to patch up my protective mental armor. This isn't the worst. If Khabri and these Order guys are right, it's only the beginning.

We're at war. This is merely a distraction.

Two of the Zmaj who aren't helping my fellow humans break off from our group. I don't know what they're doing, but it looks dumb. Dangerously stupid. They're leaping as they run, and each time they land, they slam the ground with their lochabers, making a resounding cracking sound.

They keep repeating these actions while the rest of the Zmaj gather up all the humans, several of them carrying two girls each. The ones carrying humans are leaping and gliding for long distances, landing lightly for a quick run then another leap.

"They're pulling it away," I say, suddenly getting it.

"Yes," Khabri says, speaking softly.

"Shit…" I exhale.

The zemlja bursts from the ground, but it took the bait, emerging near the two who broke off. They split, running at a forty-five-degree angle to each other, each continuing their weird dance. The zemlja waves in the air screeching, then dives back under the earth.

As it disappears below the ground, the two Zmaj angle back towards each other. They're almost to one another when one of them disappears. It's the blink of an eye. He's there, and then he's gone without a sound.

The remaining Zmaj leaps towards the spot where the other disappeared, his lochaber over his head. He thrusts the blade down, yelling a blood-curdling battle cry.

Nothing happens. He drops to his knees, leaning over the hole that swallowed his friend. His shoulders are slumped, his tail is flat on the ground, and his wings are shaking. Tears choke me, closing my throat.

I thought I was numb, my heart already shattered, but somehow seeing him there, breaks it anew.

The Zmaj don't stop running until we've put a long distance between us and where the attack happened. It's obvious they're exhausted too. They're barely running, but not a one of them complains.

When the lone Zmaj that survived encountering the zemlja catches back up to us, they come to a stop. We huddle up in silence. I've got nothing. Outside my newly repaired armor of numb, the pain of loss slithers. But inside here, I'm cold and calculating. Surviving.

After a long silence, I look at Khabri.

"What was his name?" I ask.

"I'm sorry?" he asks.

"His name?" I ask again.

"Klauth," Khabri says, understanding what I am asking at last. "And your lost male?"

"Elijah," I say, my chest constricting so tight it hurts. "His name was Elijah."

Khabri nods. "May he rest in Tajss' arms."

"Yours too," I say.

Tears sting at my eyes, but they would go with the pain that I'm holding at bay, so I don't let them have their way either.

"How much fur—"

A loud high-pitched whine grows louder and louder, cutting me off. Instinctively we all look up at once, in time to see two air machines whizz past.

"You've got to be shitting me," Petras curses.

9

KHABRI

The Invaders' ships don't stop, but there can be no doubt we've been spotted. We won't have long before they come for us. My brethren have their lochabers in hand and are forming a circle around the group, staring out and waiting for orders.

We can't win. Any fight here, in the open, with the humans to protect, we will lose. With a quick look and calculation, I estimate we're two hours from the City if we carry the humans. If they walk, it will double that.

I look at my males with a critical, judging eye. Doubt creeps into my thoughts, but then I look at her, and I know. They're exhausted, but able. They will do it because we must. We've trained for this, for worse, even.

No matter what, I can't lose her. We will protect the humans, with more of our lives if that is what it takes.

"How far?" Anna asks.

"Brethren," I say, pitching my voice to carry and inspire. "We are close, but our best chance is if we carry the humans. We must reach the City before their reinforcements arrive."

The males look one to another, doubt clear on their faces, but each of them looks at the humans, and inspiration bolsters their souls. They nod almost as one, and each of them goes to a human.

"There aren't enough of you," Anna says.

"We can run," one of the males says.

He's a scrawny male with a pinched face that is too red and pale for any human, but the determination on his face is undeniable. The other males gather around him, showing their agreement.

"You're not going to be able to keep up, Jacob," Anna says.

There's something on his face when he looks at her. He cares for her. I feel it coming off of him in waves, but it's more. There's a steel to him and these males I wouldn't have expected from humans. The kind of mettle that would have made them candidates for recruitment before the Devastation.

"We'll do our best," Jacob says. "Right, guys?"

"Yeah!" the males with him rally a cheer.

Respect swells in my chest for these males. I am proud to share a battlefield with them, but Anna is correct. They will not be able to keep up with my Zmaj. I need a better plan.

"We will split up," I say. "Humans, the City is close. The best option we have is to hold the Invaders off while you break for the safety it offers."

"Are you crazy?" Anna asks, jutting her chin angrily. "We split up and it will be worse! If they land by us, we're screwed. If you stay out here to fight, they'll overwhelm you."

A ball of warmth burns in my stomach. She's fire, heated, and it means only one thing. She cares about my survival. She wants me. I want her so badly it aches.

"Standing here fighting about it isn't going to get us anywhere," one of the males says. "We need to move."

"Right," Anna says, turning to face the human group. "This sucks, we all know it, but here's the deal. Either we man up, or we die. These bastards have killed our friends, burned our home, but are we done?"

"NO!" the humans scream, throwing their fists into the air and cheering.

Anna smiles, turning back to me and arching one delicate eyebrow.

"Very well," I say. "Brethren, help them as we can. We run."

Every one of our group finds depths of strength. The humans run, stumbling and not fast, but they're moving. At their front is Anna. I run past the others to be beside her. I help, holding her arm for support, as we run up a dune.

The humans' exhaustion is palpable. Their bodies are not conditioned for this kind of abuse, but their spirits are strong. Led by Anna.

She absorbs most of my attention. The connection between us is deep, beyond desire. The dragon melds with her. She is my everything. Her strength is unbelievable. Her leadership, the fire in her is all that any warrior could ask for in a female.

"We will have strong, warrior children," I say.

"We will what?" she asks, eyes widening.

"Our children," I say. "They will be very strong. They will be forged in the fire of your spirit and tempered by our love."

"Are you... insane?" she asks, huffing but not stopping.

"I do not understand the question," I say.

"*In-sane*," she repeats the word slowly. "Are. You. Insane. Children? Seriously? I don't even know you, and I'm sure as hell not ready to have children with you. I don't even want to date a Zmaj."

The other humans are watching the exchange between us with great interest, while the Zmaj males properly keep their attention scanning the environment for dangers.

"I am not insane," I say. "You are my mate. It is known, my

dragon has claimed you. You were sent to me by Tajss herself to be mine. By the same token, I am yours."

I take her arm to help her up the dune we're on, but she jerks it away.

"Look," she says. "I appreciate you saving us. I do. And I don't want to seem like a total bitch here, but no. Thank you, but no."

"No?"

"No," she repeats. "No children. Hell, no sex, okay? Stop looking at me like that, too. I'm not your one. I don't believe in fate, I'm not your mate, and I sure as hell am not claimed by you or claiming you for myself."

I run in silence, trying to understand her words. They contradict the look in her eyes. Her eyes burn with unspent passion. I see her looking at me when she thinks I'm not looking. I am an able male, a capable warrior. More, the claim is real. There is no mistaking it for something else.

No, Tajss intends us to be together. I am sure of it.

"Do you not have a..." I trail off trying to think of a word that would fit for humans.

They are not dragons, what are they? What is their internal guidance? Their connection to Tajss and life?

"A what? A brain? My own thoughts?"

"It is my dragon," I say. "My connection to Tajss."

"How would I be connected to Tajss? I'm not from here."

This is going bad.

"We are meant to be together," I say. "I will trust in Tajss."

"O-kay," she says, dragging the word out. "You do that."

"You are a treasure, my treasure. I will protect you, always. I will care for you, supply your every need. Your desire is my command. I am the one."

She opens her mouth when I speak, but when I continue, she

snaps it shut. Her face softens, and her frown twitches at the corners, almost becoming a smile. She shakes her head.

"You *are* insane," she says on a long exhale, but as she does, she wipes a hand across her eyes to take away the moisture resting in the corners.

The tone of her voice is different, more welcoming than before. I smile.

"If it is so," I say. "It is because your beauty has stunned me from my senses."

She gasps, swallows hard, and turns her head away. She wipes her hand across her face again, and now we run in silence. It's a better silence though. A silence born of understanding. Acceptance.

I'm not a fool. I know she doubts her fate, but that is fine. She will see, in time, I am the one. My duty now is to make sure she—and as many of her fellow humans as possible—survive to see that time arrive.

If my training in the Order has taught me anything, patience is it. We think in terms of millennia, not days or even years. Our plan to save Tajss, which is now in jeopardy, forces us to think longer. Think bigger than we ever have before.

In the Order, we had the vision of The Eye to guide us. In this, I have instinct. The finding of a mate is so native to a Zmaj that no other Zmaj would question the knowing. She is not a Zmaj though, she's human.

Perhaps they don't have the same instinct? Do they have an equivalent to our dragon? That manifestation of our primal selves? It is so core to what a Zmaj is, I don't think any of us have questioned the presence of it in the humans.

Our dragon is the core of who we, as Zmaj and as males, are. It is, like all things, good and bad but yet neither. It is our potential and our drive. Unlike my brethren, my training has allowed me to stay in control of the negative aspects of it, the bijass.

The bijass is the dragon's smokey breath covering over memory, forcing us to live in the moment we are in by stealing away moments that came before. It saves us from knowing all that we have done, from living with the losses and the pain by making those memories vague. It is our drive towards primality. Our basest instincts and the drive to dominate the world around us.

The dragon is our connection to Tajss itself.

I wish I had time to explore this further. I want to know her, to understand everything about her. Anticipation quivers within me, impatient for her to share all with me as I will share all with her. We will be as one. Raising our beautiful children together.

A roaring whine interrupts my thoughts. Invaders.

My Zmaj form a barrier around the humans, closing in the stragglers. Four transport ships whiz overhead. The ships speed through the air in a tight formation. They pass us then come to a stop, hovering in the air three dozen strides away.

Murmurs of fear and building panic rise from the humans, but the Zmaj are looking at me, waiting for orders.

"Sir?" Pachua asks.

We're close. The City dome sparkles on the horizon.

"We run," I say. "Warriors, help the humans."

Panic overtakes the humans and they run. My Zmaj form a line behind the running crowd, ready to help any who slow down. Anna is still standing, staring at me.

"We're not going to make it," she says.

"We don't have a choice," I say. "When they close with us, my warriors will fight to buy you time to get your people into the City."

She swallows. Her lips and hands tremble as she frowns.

"You... can't," she says, her words coming out tight.

"I will protect you and your people," I say.

She walks closer and time stops. No matter the impending

danger, the world is nothing but the two of us. She stops a hand's width away. I feel her warmth and her breath on my scales. Desire is a hard knot in my core.

"I don't know you," she whispers, one trembling hand reaching across the distance and coming to rest on my chest.

Her hand is warm. So warm, kind, my hearts gallop at her touch. Blood rushes to my head making me dizzy, and my mouth is dry as the sand. I want to touch her, but I don't dare.

"You will," I whisper.

"Fate, right," she says.

Her eyes glisten brightly. Her lips are so full and lush, it takes all my will to not taste them. I want, with every fiber of my being, to lay my claim on them. The dragon roars, pushing me to do it, but she is not ready. I will not.

"Yes," I say. "We are meant for one another."

"Don't die," she says. "I want to find out."

I'm hanging on every word. My chest constricts until my hearts can't beat. I'm held in this magical moment with her. Nothing else matters. She withdraws her hand and time rushes forward, my hearts working double time to catch up.

"I won't. I promise. Now run," I order, boldly hooking an arm around her waist and helping her.

We catch the others as I hear the sounds of pursuit on the ground. The ships have unloaded dozens of Invaders. Their boots crunch loudly as they run after us. I let Anna go to help another human who stumbles and falls. She keeps running while I carry the fallen human until he's gotten his bearings again and can run on his own.

My warriors do the same, helping one human, then another. Keeping them moving forward. Every time I glance back, the Invaders are closing in, but slowly. We're climbing one of the last and biggest dunes before we'll see the City. The sight of it will reinvigorate the humans.

The crowd stops at the top of the dune. No one moves. Even my warriors have come to a stop.

"What is this?" I yell, doubling my speed.

When I crest the dune, my hearts stop.

The land before the dome is a flat run from this dune right up to it. Now there isn't an open space between the dune and the dome. Invaders fill the space, surrounding the dome, stretching as far as I can see.

It looks like thousands of them. I look over my shoulder and our pursuers are about to catch us.

"Prepare!" I yell, drawing my lochaber and turning to face the threat.

I look at Anna and see the horror on her face.

"I'm sorry," I say. "I don't think I can keep my promise."

LADON

THE PAIN IN MY CHEST HASN'T STOPPED SINCE I LEFT HER. I continue ignoring it the best I can. I'm doing what must be done to save them. It would be easier if she'd agree to leave with me, let all these others fend for themselves.

"I don't know anything about cryogenics," Addison says.

"What is that?" Visidion asks.

"Keeping people in a frozen state, but alive," she says. "That's what it sounds like they've done."

"There must be a way to wake them up," I say. "If they are Zmaj, we need them. We need more warriors."

"There were rumors of this place," Visidion says. "Before. It was a place of great evil."

"Evil or not, we can use it," I say.

Calista should be here. My arms ache to hold her.

"Look, I don't know about evil and all that," Luke, one of the humans says. "I do know we don't know anything about that place. That makes it dangerous. We already had a sickness come out of there. What else we willing to risk for this? What's the upside?"

"The upside is we win," I snap.

"What is it you think we're winning?" Luke says.

He doesn't back down, but the color on his face pales at my outburst. I struggle against the surge of red swelling through my thoughts. The bijass wants to crush these people who would dare stand against me. The other half a dozen human males mutter and shift but no one speak out. Visidion watches with cool, calculating eyes.

"Ladon," Sverre says, shaking his head. "These are our allies. There is no reason to be angry."

"None of you understand!" I yell, slamming my fist into the open palm of my hand. "This is real. We are in danger, gathered here in one place. It's terrible strategy."

"What strategy?" Shidan asks. "This isn't a strategy. We're living."

"Exactly," I say. Anger pulses in time with my hearts. Thrumming through my veins, violent, discordant music keeping me on edge. "None of you are seeing the danger we are in. I will not fail to protect my family. I will do whatever it takes."

Even if that means kidnapping them and forcing them to go away with me.

Everyone watches me but no one argues further. Luke clears his throat then shrugs.

"All right," Luke says. "So what are we going to try to accomplish, then?"

"If the stories are true," Visidion says. "This bunker was for cutting-edge research."

"It was," Archion says, speaking for the first time.

"What does the Order know?" I ask, narrowing my eyes.

Archion's face is as blank as the empty sands.

"Experiments that were done there were terrible," he says. "The virus—"

He stops, cutting himself short.

"The virus, what? What is it you know?" I ask, moving into his space, raising my tail between my wings.

He squares his shoulders, meeting my advance, but overall he remains calm.

"It may have been one of their experiments," he says.

"Why didn't you say so?" Rick, another of the human males, asks.

"Because I don't know," Archion says, not taking his eyes off mine. "It is a guess, at best."

"You *knew*," I hiss through clenched teeth.

"No," he says, not backing down.

The bijass swells, surging against my control, assaulting rationality. There is whispering in my head. He is not to be trusted. I should destroy him for withholding this information. Visidion places a hand on my shoulder. He doesn't try to force me back or move me, but it draws my attention to him.

"I am myself," Visidion says the words soft, a gentle reminder.

"I'm not Tribe," I say.

"No," Visidion agrees. "But you are a warrior."

I want him to fight me. I want someone to fight. A target. Something I can hit or punch. Something I can make obey, but none of these males are giving it to me. Lacking something to resist, the bijass recedes, leaving my muscles trembling.

"If we wear suits, we could go in and look around, at least," Mischa, a small human male, offers. "What can it hurt?"

"I saw the missiles," Shidan says. "But are they working? Do we know how to launch them?"

Suspicious, I look at Archion. "Can you?"

Archion frowns and hesitates before answering. "Probably."

"Then it's settled," I say. "We are going to the bunker. We will explore and find all the data we can."

"I don't want Addison to come along," Visidion says. "Melchior is not here to go along. It is not right to put his mate—"

"I can damn well speak for myself," Addison says.

"I understand, but—" Visidion says, turning to her.

"But nothing. What I do or don't do isn't up to Melchior."

"He should have some say," Visidion says.

I watch the other Zmaj as they shift uncomfortably with this conversation. None of them disagree, but they don't want to speak up against Addison, knowing that she will tell their mates. I'm already in trouble with Calista, and I agree too.

"No," I say.

"Excuse me?" Addison asks, whirling on me.

"No," I say. "You will not go."

"And who is it you suddenly have an iota of a chance at understanding these cryogenic machines?" she asks. Her eyes are cold daggers piercing into me but I'm not backing down.

"The missiles are the goal," I say. "As everyone keeps reminding me, we're not under invasion right now."

"Then why are you in such a rush?" Addison asks.

The question is the same one on everybody's mind. Their eyes bore into me, and the bijass rises in answer once more.

"They're in the sky!" I yell. "Waiting. Ready to pounce. Look at us," I motion my arm around the room. "We've all gathered together like we're ready to be picked off. It's not a matter of if, it's a matter of when!"

"Ladon, they wanted the meteorite glass," Timothy, another human says. "They're done gone now that the showers are over."

"No, they aren't!"

I glare at the crowd around me. They're fools. Blind. Refusing to see the truth that I see. Pent-up frustration and rage thrum through my muscles. In my mind's eye I see Calista and Illadon. Laughing, happy—then I lose them. I've been dreaming this scenario over and over. Now I see it here, wide awake.

"Something terrible is going to happen," I say. "I know it."

The Zmaj exchange a look with each other, and the humans do the same.

"He could be right," Luke says. "We don't know what they wanted."

Every beat of my hearts is pain. Pain of a loss that hasn't happened, that I can't let happen. Calista is my world. I must protect her and our son. I know I'm right. This irritation, like an itch in my brain I can't scratch, won't stop.

Sverre comes and places a hand on my shoulder.

"Ladon," he says. "You have become my brother in arms and in spirit. I am at your side, and I believe you. We will do what we must."

Murmurs of agreement come from those assembled.

"Good or evil is in the intention of the user," Visidion says. "My memories of this place are vague, and as I recall, they were but whispered myths and rumors even then. No one knew if this place was real, but now we do. We know it exists, and we know that things happened there for some unknown purpose."

"They were preparing for war," Archion says.

"War? Then?" Visidion asks.

"Yes," Archion says. "The war that we all knew was to come. The war for the soul of Tajss."

Silence follows his pronouncement. The members of the Order I've interacted with all love their cryptic pronouncements. As if they want to be seen as visionaries. I'm not buying the act, but I see its effect on the others, especially the humans.

"The soul of Tajss?" I ask. "What does that even mean? I'm not fighting for some mystical soul of the planet—I fight for my family."

"As it should be," Archion says, not elaborating further.

I'd really like to punch him in the face, but it would accomplish nothing. If anything, it would further anger Calista. I hear her admonishment in my head, which is enough to stop me from taking action.

"So we're agreed? We go to the bunker?" I ask.

"Yes," Visidion says.

"I'm going, too," Addison says.

The Zmaj suddenly become interested in the ground, leaving Visidion and me to handle her.

"No," I say.

"You can't stop me," Addison says. "You're going to need me."

"No," I say.

"Addison, let us go first," Visidion says. "We will bring you once we've done further exploration."

She purses her lips and clenches her fists then opens them and sighs. "Fine."

"Very well," Visidion says. "I want this to be a small task force. Archion, the Order seems to have better understanding of pre-Devastation tech, will you go?"

He's nicer than I would be. I'd order him to go and let him shove his Order.

"We do and I will," Archion says.

"Good. Then we will leave tomorrow mor—"

THUH-BOOM!

I'm thrown into Visidion. Entangled, we fall to the ground together. Debris falls from the ceiling, pelting my back. My ears are ringing, and sounds are distant, but people are screaming.

"Calista!" I roar, fighting my way free of Visidion.

A quick glance shows no one here is seriously hurt, and I'm out the door.

My nightmares thrust to the fore, consuming my thoughts with random still images. Calista bleeding. Illadon lying lifeless, face down. My hearts pound as I race through the City streets. People rush up and down the streets screaming, covered in dirt, some bleeding, but I don't see anyone seriously hurt.

I run faster. Slamming down one foot after another, powering my way forward. I open my wings to bound from one leap to the next.

"What happened?" a human male asks, stumbling into my path.

He's covered in dirt and blood trickles down his head. He's staring wide-eyed as he blocks my path.

"Out of the way!" I yell.

"Help her," he says, pointing, shaking his head. "Please!"

The pleading in his voice cuts through the noise in my head. I follow his pointing hand to a building. A plume of dirt drifts out of the broken window, and past the ringing in my ears, a distant female screams.

Cursing, I run for the building. The dirt obscures my sight, and I stumble over debris, blindly working my way towards the sound of the female's voice. The male is right behind. He curses and yells too.

Emerging from the roiling dust cloud into an open floor space, I find her. A beam has fallen from the ceiling, pinning her legs. She has long, dark hair, and for an instant I see Calista. The dragon roars, and I can't hold it in. I roar as I rush forward.

The female stops screaming, looking at me in wide-eyed terror. This is not Calista. It is not Calista.

I grab the beam, bend my knees, and lift with all I have. The movement causes creaks and groans, and more debris falls from the ceiling. It lifts off of her, but she is lying still, unable to move.

"Help her!" I bark at the male.

He stumbles forward and grabs her arms, pulling her free. Something in the ceiling cracks loud enough to be heard over the ringing in my ears. We need to get out of here. I grab both the humans, one in each arm, and run.

Rumbling begins behind us, and then the ceiling crashes down as we emerge. A blast of air slams into my back, and I'm thrown to the ground with the humans. I climb to my feet and help the male up.

"Take her to the medical," I order. "Can you do this?"

"Y-ye-yes," he stutters.

"Go!"

A bright light flashes, leaving afterimages on my eyes, and then the boom sounds again. The sound hits my chest with a palpable force, making me step back. The human male falls on his ass.

I do not have time for this. After running to him, I get him on his feet. Holding him by his shoulders, I stoop to look into his eyes.

"GO!" I yell again, and he nods.

Only now do I look up, and my stomach clenches as my muscles thrum with pent-up energy. A huge ship hangs over the City, and it is firing on the dome.

I was right.

No pleasure comes with being right, only horror. I do not know where my mate or my child are. Terror comes with that thought, and I'm running. I run faster than I've ever run before.

She is okay. They are fine. They are fine. They are fine.

I repeat the mantra every time my foot hits the ground. Buildings blur as I run. Another flash and bang but I ignore it. Reaching Calista and Illadon is all that matters.

I turn a corner, and ahead is the City center. The fountain looms large. She should be here. Dozens of humans mill around the streets in confusion. They see me charge towards them and part, letting me pass through unimpeded.

"CALISTA!" I roar, spreading my wings and leaping to gain height.

I don't hear her, but I feel her. I'm drawn to the left, so I turn and keep running. I call for her, over and over, but as I run, my dragon guides me. Pulling and guiding me towards her.

"Ladon!"

My hearts pound faster when I hear her voice. There's a large pile of rubble. I see her hand rise above it, and then her head appears. She is covered in dirt as she rises into view. I race up the side of the loose debris, leaping from one perch to the next.

Illadon has his arms around her neck and legs around her waist. She stumbles forward, and I catch them before she can fall.

I squeeze them to my chest. I never want to let them go. I should never have left them alone. I should have made her leave. The war I felt coming is here.

"Ladon," she sobs. "We have to help the others."

"You first," I say.

Even now she is concerned with others. Her heart is so expansive she isn't even concerned with herself.

"I'm fine," she says. "We're fine."

"Where is Rverre? I have to find her!" Illadon declares, worming his way out of our grasp.

The instant his feet touch down, he's running, bounding down the side of the rubble, tiny wings carrying him away too fast.

"Illadon!" Calista screams.

I tighten my grip on her and leap into the air. I'm larger and more skilled at gliding, allowing me to land in front of our son, cutting off his route.

"Out of the way!" he yells, raising his fists. "I must save her!"

A sense of pride in my son swells so big it feels as if I will explode. He is a true warrior, a male in every sense of the word.

"We will, son," I say. "Stay with your mother. We'll find them."

He frowns deeply, but nods. "Now?"

"Yes," I say, setting Calista onto her own feet. "Do you know where Jolie was?"

"She was on duty at the food stores," Calista says. "Rverre should be with her."

Another flash of light is followed by a boom drowning out any words we would say. I point towards the food stores. Calista nods in understanding, grabs Illadon's hand, and they run that way.

I have to find out how bad this is. Will the dome hold to the assault? What else are they bringing to bear? Too many questions, and I need answers now.

I watch Calista run, hesitating, not wanting to leave them. I force myself to blink, then I turn and run for the edge of the City, but my heart is with them.

Humans clog the streets of my city. Some are hurt, most are wandering the streets with no purpose, all are scared.

Fear is in the air. An acrid scent of sweat tinged with something sour. It assaults my nose, making breathing harder. I make my way through them, yelling and pushing when I must. Many of them move as if they're in a daze, staring up at the dome and watching the ship assaulting us.

If the ship were my only concern it'd be enough, but I know it's not all. Instinct screams that it's not a single attack. It's war.

As the edge of the city comes into view and the dome is in sight, I stop dead in my tracks. The airlock guards have formed a barricade on the street blocking the path between two buildings. Beyond the dome, the parts of my nightmares my waking mind refused to look at have come to life.

Hundreds if not thousands of Invaders stand in formation outside the dome. Waiting.

"How many?" I ask the human male kneeling behind the barrier.

They've gathered broken furniture, stones, and beams to create a sense of safety that is nothing more than an illusion. If the dome comes down, it's over.

"Too many to count," he says, pressing his lips together.

I climb over the barrier and walk to the dome. A thousand pairs of eyes lock onto me as I pace the dome. Too many. We can't win this fight. If we're going to stand a chance, we have to do something unexpected.

They're standing in neat squares with fifty Invaders per group. Cold, yellow eyes stare ahead, unfeeling and uncaring. They follow orders, and that's it.

Something tugs at my thoughts, an old mostly forgotten memory. They're unborn. While I study them, I focus on the memory, trying to understand.

Unborn? The fog of my past blows away and the memory comes clear. They're clones. Made in laboratories for no other purpose than to wage war. I fought them during the war that led to the Devastation.

Waves of cold emanate from my stomach. They are a terrifying opponent. The group in front of me suddenly turns an about face, looking out into the desert. Something has pulled their attention, and I look out too.

"Oh, no," I exhale.

A mixed group of humans and Zmaj stands at the top of the dune beyond them. They'll be killed if we don't do something.

My dragon roars, and I let it out in a full bellow. I can't let these people die at the hands of these monsters. A crushing weight settles on my shoulders, and I know. It's up to me.

CALISTA

"HURRY UP, MOMMY!" ILLADON YELLS, TUGGING MY ARM.

Another flash of light causes me to jump before the sound of it even happens. Illadon doesn't slow down, bowing his head and running faster. Outside the food storage, several people are grouped. They're covered in dirt, some bleeding, and all of them look shell-shocked.

"RVERRE!" Illadon screams, his voice cracking.

He lets go of my hand, freeing both of his to push people out of his way.

"JOLIE!" I yell, panic rising.

She should be here. Illadon clears the way, and I'm following in his wake. He's seven, which doesn't seem possible. He's big. I can't say he's big for his age since he's half-Zmaj. He's probably small for a Zmaj, but who knows? He's pushing hard on five feet tall and he's well-muscled. He's a miniature of his dad, except his face. I see a lot of me in his face. His nose is softer, like mine.

"RVERRE!" Illadon calls to his friend again.

"I think they're inside," someone yells to be heard over the noise.

"Thank you," I say, rushing to try to keep up with Illadon.

Bert stumbles out the open door holding his head. He wavers and trips as he emerges, and Illadon catches him. Illadon pushes Bert back onto his feet, gripping his arms.

"Have you seen Rverre?" Illadon asks.

"Rverre?" Bert asks, shaking his head. When he takes his hand away there is a nasty cut on his forehead and blood drips into his eyes. "Inside, still, I think."

Illadon doesn't bother answering, he lets Bert go and rushes into the building. Smoke is drifting out the door, and now I smell something is burning.

"What's happened?" Bert asks, seeing me. "Earthquake?"

"Invaders," I say. "I have to get Jolie."

He pales and nods, moving out of my way. Inside the building smoke curls along the ceiling. I crouch and run. Illadon is nowhere to be seen. There is a hall ahead that leads to where the food prep work is done. I assume that's where he went, so I go that way. The smoke grows thicker as I head down the hall. It isn't long before I hear voices.

"JOLIE! ILLADON!" I yell.

Yelling makes me inhale smoke which leaves me coughing. It's stinging my eyes, and they fill with tears trying to wash it away. Crouching lower, I'm almost bent in half as I waddle-run down the hall towards the voices. I reach the door to the prep area.

"I'll get you!" Illadon yells from the other side.

I grab the handle, my heart in my throat with fear of what he's going to do. As soon as I touch the handle, my skin sizzles and I jerk my hand free.

"Shit!" I curse, looking at my hand.

It's not bad, but the handle being that hot is. I use the hem of my shirt to wrap cloth around my hand to protect myself, then try the door again. It works. The door opens.

Flames roar out of the door. I stumble back. The flames are the fingers of giant hands, grasping the wall, trying to break free. Shielding my eyes beyond the flames I see Illadon. Jolie and Rverre are cut off by a burning beam that has fallen.

"Illadon, get out of here!" Jolie screams. "I'll find a way, get out before more comes down!"

As if in response, another sonic boom rattles the building. Dirt and debris falls, and a crack races down the wall. There's no time to waste. Shielding my face with an arm, I run through the roiling flames engulfing the door frame. The heat steals my breath.

"Illadon, run!" I order.

"No," he says. He's looking up down and around with fast movements of his head. "Not without her."

"Illadon get out, please!" Rverre yells. She's clinging to Jolie's side.

Flames stretch higher. The ceiling is a churning inferno, and the flames on the beam are stretching to join their brothers. It feels as if my skin is peeling back before the onslaught of waves of hot.

CRACK!

A flaming hunk of the ceiling falls and explodes as it hits the ground, sending glowing embers dancing in the air. Then I spot a chance.

"Jolie, the far end!" I yell.

She doesn't wait, dragging Rverre with her, she runs. Illadon and I pace her the length of the beam.

"I see it," Jolie says.

A long metal table rests against this wall. Flaming debris covers it, but they can crawl underneath it. The table has created a small save haven.

Jolie grabs Rverre and throws her through the wall of flames. She screams, but lands underneath the table safely.

"Come to me, honey, come on," I coax her, reaching for her.

She has to crawl under the table far enough so I can reach her. The beam and its flames rests on top of it. She looks back for her mother, then scrambles ahead on all fours. The moment my fingers touch her, I jerk her out and spin her around.

"Illadon, get her out of here, now," I order.

"Mom, Jolie," he argues.

"No!" I yell. "Protect Rverre, I'll help Jolie."

He's torn, I see it on his face, but he grabs Rverre and runs out. When I whip around, the flames are higher. It's going to be much harder for Jolie to get past them without being severely burned. The crawl space under that table wasn't a problem for Rverre but as small as Jolie is, she's not that small.

"Come on Jolie," I say. "You can do this. Come on."

She shakes her head back and forth. Tears stream down her face but I see the truth. Rverre is safe and she's giving up.

"I can't," she cries.

"You can," I say. "You have to. I can't do this without you."

"I can't," she says, moving back and forth.

She rocks in place, backing away from the flames that are consuming more and more. Debris falls from the ceiling making the passage tighter.

"Jolie, damn it, we don't have time for this. Do it! Do it now!"

"Tell Sverre and Rverre I love them," she bawls. "Run, Calista, I'm sorry. I love you!"

"Don't you do this to me!" I yell. "No. You don't get out of this that easy. Do it or I'm coming in there after you."

"I'm sorry," she wraps her arms around herself and twists from side to side. "I'm sorry Calista, I love you, but I'm sorry."

"You're going to be sorry. I'm going to kick your ass when we get out of this, now do it!"

She drops to her knees, bowing her head.

No matter the heat and the fire, cold penetrates me to my core. She's trapped. Another loud crack and more of the ceiling falls. The wall behind her is peeling and cracking.

"No!" I scream. "Get up. Get up and try, damn it. No!"

She looks up. Her beautiful face is flushed with burns. She looks around, then shakes her head. Something cracks again, and then the wall behind her explodes.

"NO-O-O-O-O-O-O!" I scream, tearing my vocal cords.

Light and fresh air stream through the wall. I rub my eyes, unable to believe it. Sverre scoops Jolie into his arms and turns back to the opening he created. He pauses and looks over his shoulder.

"RUN!" he yells.

I don't wait. My throat burns and my lungs scream as I try to get oxygen. In the hall, I drop to my knees and crawl. The smoke is too thick to see my way out, and I can't breathe.

My head is swimming. I'm dizzy. My arms shake with the effort of holding myself up and trying to move.

Blackness closes in. A bit farther. Almost there.

I drop to the floor. The tile is a welcome coolness on my face. Throwing my arms in front of myself, I try to get a grasp on anything. When my fingers hook on something, I pull myself forward a few more inches.

A little rest. A moment. Get some air.

I huff for air, but it's filled with smoke, making me cough more. The blackness swirls in again, closing its grasp.

Can't fall asleep.

Must. Stay. Awake.

My arms are grabbed, and then I'm sliding across the floor. In a moment, I'm in the daylight.

"MOM!" Illadon yells, his cherubic face swimming into sight.

"She will be fine," Sverre says. His rough hands cup my face then lift my head.

Water touches my lips, and greedily I gulp it. Then my diaphragm constricts, and I sputter and cough, spewing water down the front of myself.

Someone helps me sit up, and I cough more. When I take a breath at last, my throat and lungs burn. It hurts, but I'm alive.

"Jolie," I say, trying to climb to my feet.

"I'm okay," she says from beside me.

She's there. I throw myself around her, squeezing her with all I've got. She returns my hug, and we hold each other for I don't know how long. When I finally let her go, I hold her face in my hands.

"Don't you *ever* do that again!" I say, tears streaming.

"I'm sorry," she says.

"You damn well should be," I say.

"It's not safe here," Sverre says. "We must get everyone to the bunkers under the city."

"The electrical tunnels?" Jolie asks.

"Yes, it will be safest," Sverre says.

"Ladon went to help," I say. "I have to find him."

Sverre stands and looks over the gathered crowd of humans. He stares down the mostly empty street beyond our huddle of humanity.

"He was right," Sverre says softly.

A cold knife stabs into my heart. The chills race down my limbs, driven in by his words. Ladon was right. He saw this coming, somehow. He wanted to take us away, but I said no.

"Jolie, can you lead these people to the tunnels?" I ask.

"Yes, but what about you?" she asks.

"I'm going with Sverre to find Ladon and help as many as I can," I say. "I need you to take Illadon."

"I'm big enough to go with you," Illadon complains.

"Yes," I agree. "You are, but then who will take care of Jolie? I'm taking Sverre with me."

"Oh," Illadon says. "Right. I can do this."

Jolie and I stand up. We stare into each other's eyes for a long time, then pull each other into a tight embrace.

"I love you," I whisper.

"I love you," she says. "Thank you."

The lump in my throat won't let me say anything more, so I pat her back, then step a bit away, rubbing my forearm over my eyes. Her eyes are glistening too, but she doesn't speak more either. She reaches out her hands, taking Rverre's and Illadon's hands.

"Everyone follow me! We're going to safety," Jolie yells to be heard by the crowd.

One last look at me then she is leading the crowd away.

"Which way?" I ask Sverre.

"The dome," he says.

I nod and we run. He could outpace me easily, but he does me the courtesy of slowing to my speed. My poor body has been through hell already. Every muscle hurts, and my lungs feel like I inhaled some of the fire and it's trapped in there.

We pass small groups of humans, and we stop with each one, giving them directions to get into the tunnels. It's a smart move. The buildings of the City are in bad shape. Even the ones we've been working to repair and make livable aren't ready for this kind of abuse.

And if the dome falls...

I shy away from the thought. It can't. That's it.

It feels like it takes forever, but we come into sight of the dome at last. A large group of human men and several Zmaj are at the airlock, surrounding Ladon. The relief of seeing him is overwhelmed by what I see beyond the dome.

So many of them. I stop dead in my tracks and stare. "Shit."

Ladon and the group are looking out, but it doesn't look like the siege outside the dome has their attention. Ladon points beyond. I track across the hundreds of Invaders standing in perfect formation to what he is indicating.

It can't be. I squeeze my eyes shut, balling my hands into fists so tight my nails dig into my palms.

"Sverre, do you see that?" I ask, not opening my eyes.

I'm praying. Praying that I didn't see what I thought I saw. Please, by all that is holy, please don't be.

"It is the miners," Sverre says.

My shoulder muscles tense so tight it makes my head hurt. I want to curse, to scream, to make it not be them out there. I open my eyes again and burst into a run.

"No one has to go," Ladon is saying when I get close enough. "But if we don't, they will die."

"We have to try," Shidan says.

"We're going," Adam, one of the human guards says. "We got a plan besides running out there and trying to look real scary?"

Ladon sees me and his mouth snaps shut before he answers. The look on his face makes my heart ache. Resignation tinged with pain, but more than anything, his love for me burns in his eyes. The moment our eyes meet the connection between us clicks. I know what he's thinking, like I always do.

He's regretting what he's about to do. He doesn't want to upset me. Even more, he doesn't want to leave me, but he can't let them die without trying to save them. It's who he is. A warrior, yes, but beyond that, he's a man of honor. His sense of honor is so deep, so fundamental to who he is, I can't stand in his way. If I try, I'd be betraying my love for him.

We both swallow, and I nod. He nods too, then returns his attention to those waiting around him. He holds out his hand flat and points at it, giving his plan. He's a leader in his element. I'm barely able to stay standing. My knees are weak and shaking. My head is spinning, and my eyes sting with unshed tears.

"Don't die," I whisper.

Ladon looks up, meets my eyes and smiles. His eyes sparkle. The men break for the airlock. I want, with all my heart, to tell him no. Don't do it. Keep them all inside where we're safe. Let those outside fend for themselves!

Instead I keep my jaw clenched and say nothing. What kind of person would it make me? I'm trembling. Sverre is gone with the others. They burst out of the airlock with Ladon in the lead. He's working his lochaber so fast it's a blur. My men, for they are all mine really, charge the Invaders.

The Invaders charge my guys, and even though the sound is dampened by the dome, the clash is resounding. Chaos ensues as the two groups clash. One of the Zmaj falls, and my heart stops. I run to the dome, pressing my face against it, trying to see through the mashing of bodies who it was.

Ladon leaps into the air, swinging his lochaber in a wide arc and relief rushes through my body. Instantly in its wake, I'm nauseated. If it wasn't Ladon, whose mate went down? My lips tremble. I press my hand to the dome. Tears pour down my face, but I don't wipe them away.

I don't dare blink. I'm bearing witness to an act of heroism such as comes once in a lifetime. Why heroism and death come hand in hand, I'll never understand.

I don't know what possesses me, but I'm singing through my tears. An ancient song that my mom used to sing while she was doing housework. It comes unbidden and falls from my cracked lips as my heart breaks, shattering further with every beat.

Soldier keep on marchin' on,

The Invaders mob my guys. A shape flies up into the air, thrown by one of the Invaders. The Invader raises its sword, impaling the form as it comes down.

Head down 'till the work is done,

I can't look away. I'm a lone, cold witness, and I won't dishonor these men. Adam. Adam is gone. He was the one they threw into the air, and he's now a broken doll.

Waiting on that morning sun,

Sverre is thrown against the dome. Six Invaders close on him and he attacks with renewed ferocity.

Solider keep on marchin' on.

It's no good. They're going to lose. I can't hold back. I slam my fists against the dome and scream.

"Come back! Get out of there!"

They don't. The miners have Zmaj with them. They must be from the Order or something because they're not Tribe. The Invaders' force is split as they deal with both groups, but they outnumber my guys ten to one, if not more.

Stamping my feet and pounding my fists, I scream. I'm so helpless. There's nothing I can do.

"It doesn't end like this! We don't end like this!"

The ground rumbles. I look up but there's no flash, so it's not the ship bombing. Dirt bounces up and down on the street, and the rumbling is louder. Cracks form in the tarmac of the road. Loud cracks sound from the buildings behind me.

What fresh hell is—

Off to the left, an entire group of Invaders is thrown high into the air. A dust cloud filled with bodies and debris rises with them,, blocking my sight. Something happened, but what?

The mass of bodies separated from me by the thin barrier of the dome disentangles, The Invaders step back then run towards their companions, bringing their weapons to bear. An ear-splitting screech, so loud I drop to my knees covering my ears.

"Come on!" Ladon's voice roars over the commotion.

The dust cloud is rolling over, obscuring my vision, but I see him. The mining group is running down the dune towards the

City. The Invaders have separated and are grouping up off to the far side, but they're not paying attention to my guys. It makes no sense except...

I see it.

It thrusts up, reaching so high into the sky it looks taller than the dome itself. I fall back onto my ass and crabwalk backwards. Cold fear grips my guts. I've seen zemlja before but never one this big. It's not big. It's massive.

This monster is bigger than the skyscraper buildings behind me, and it is tearing its way through the Invaders.

The Zmaj are all carrying two humans each and racing for the airlock, taking advantage of the moment.

"Yeah!" Illadon yells, suddenly appearing next to me.

"What?!" I scream, leaping to my feet.

"Do you see that!" Illadon asks, pointing and jumping up and down.

"Why... how... what are you doing here?"

"Helping," he says, running to the airlock.

I run after him, but he reaches it first, punching in the code to open it. The first Zmaj crowd in as many as they can. I don't have time to properly reprimand my son, right now I have to save them.

"Move," I bark, pushing him to one side.

I know the code, what is it? I rack my brain trying to remember... it's... damn it. Oh!

I punch the override code in, and both sides of the airlock open, letting the entire group rush in without having to wait for it to cycle through.

Once they're all in, I shut the doors, then stare out at the Invaders. Their massive ship is moving into place over the zemlja. It's not going to be able to stand up to a blast from that thing.

"No!" I scream, rooting for the monster.

It twists, and then burrows into the ground fast. Just like that, it's over. The Invaders are in a total disarray. I turn to the survivors and Ladon pushes his way free. He sweeps me up in one arm and his lips smash to mine.

"Gross!" Illadon exclaims.

"What are you doing here?" Ladon asks, cutting our kiss short.

"I came to help," Illadon says. "I made sure everyone was safe in the tunnels, and then I came to fight."

"Son, you are very brave," Ladon says kneeling before him. "But this is an important lesson for you to learn."

"Yeah?" Illadon asks.

"A warrior must obey orders," Ladon says softly.

He's not angry, if anything he's beaming with pride, but he doesn't let that stop him from being a father. A damn good father that I am so relieved is here with us.

"Yes, daddy," Illadon says, head bowed.

His horns are getting bigger, I note. Inane things you notice after the rush of the adrenaline is gone.

"You understand?" Ladon asks. "The first and most important rule, son."

"Yes, daddy," Illadon says, kicking at the street.

"Good," Ladon says, pulling Illadon into an embrace. He lifts him up and shifts him to his hip, then holds his arm open towards me.

I step into his waiting arm, press my head to his chest, and I break down.

ANNA

"IT'S BEEN FIVE DAYS," I SAY, STARING AT THE SMALL PORTIONS of food on my plate.

This is the only meal I'll have for the day, and I feel guilty eating even this much. As if I'm a thief or something. I don't belong here. None of us do. The small group of survivors from the mining settlement have kept to ourselves, mostly.

It's not like the people of the City haven't been welcoming. If they hadn't come out to save us, we wouldn't be here. Not a one of them has said a cross word. But there are the looks. Momentary, passing, but all of us have caught them. We don't belong here.

"Five days in hell is still five days in hell," Isla mutters.

My stomach grumbles, so I eat the small portion of food. It's not like I really want it anyway. I'm nauseated, and my head hurts so badly I wish it would explode and get it over with.

"When are they going to do something?" Aurora asks.

We all know who she's talking about. The Invaders stopped bombing after the zemlja attacked. Since then, they haven't done anything except sit outside and wait. Implacably. Pitilessly. And why not? They've got all the time in the world, but we don't.

Rosalind put the City on strict rationing immediately, but no one is stupid enough to think that's going to be enough. There isn't enough food stored inside the dome to feed us all. Any way you go, you end up at the same dead-end road. The Invaders apparently know it too, so they're waiting us out.

The door to the dining area opens and I jump. Khabri and two of the Order Zmaj walk in. He carries himself like he's in charge. Arrogant, in control, used to the universe and everyone around him bending to his will without question.

His eyes land on me and I drop my gaze quickly. The heat in my belly soothes the nausea, which I appreciate, but I'm not going to stare at him for relief. Though, the more I look at him, the more I like it.

He's got a good face. Imperious. His nose is strong, and so is his jaw, but his high brow is what really gets me. I love a man with a high forehead. Not a receding-hairline brow, but those that have that tallness to it. It makes him look intelligent. Which he is, or seems to be, if not for the insistence he and I are fated to be together.

"Fate, schmate," I mutter.

Sophia is sitting next to me, and she doesn't miss it. "He likes you."

"You think?" I ask. "What gave it away? When he told me we were going to make beautiful babies together?" Sophia's cheeks flush bright red, and she looks away. I didn't mean to embarrass her, so I place a hand on her leg and squeeze. "Sorry."

"It's okay," she shrugs. "We're all on edge."

"On edge to say the least," Harper chimes in. "You ever think about it?"

"About what?" I ask.

She drops her voice to a whisper and says, "You know," darting her eyes toward Khabri.

"No!" I lie.

Nope, those nighttime fantasies aren't me thinking about it. That's my subconscious running away with itself. Nothing to do with me… except for the warmth stoking in my belly, and the way my throat is all dry and scratchy.

The way he looked at me outside the City. Facing certain death and still his only thought was of saving me. No concern for his own life. Everything shifted in that moment. I saw him in a way I'd never imagined.

Yet, he's a Zmaj. Alien. Different. Can I let myself feel this way about him? What will my friends think? It's confusing, but my body absolutely responds when he's around.

Obviously, other girls have fallen in love with Zmaj. That's what started the rift among us humans, but I never believed it. At least, I never really believed it. I was scared. I snort, *was* scared? I'm still scared. A knife's edge away from terrified.

Which begs the question, would I feel this way about him if I weren't? He can talk about fate all he wants, but I don't believe in it. Maybe he should hook up with Morgana—she's the spiritualist of our group.

It's so hard to sort out my feelings when every pounding in my head blasts away whatever train of thought I'm on. Rubbing my temples, I lean on the table and try to breathe my way through a fresh wave of nausea.

"I don't feel good," Maeve says, rising from her seat.

Before she makes another move, she collapses onto the table.

"Maeve!" I join the others in calling her name.

We lift her up onto the table, shoving our plates out of the way, and lay her down. Sweat beads on her pale face and she's murmuring something. Then she starts shaking violently. Jacob and Liam throw themselves on top of her, holding her down and keeping her from falling off the table. I grab her head to stop her from banging it onto the table over and over.

"Mageir," Khabri barks, suddenly at my side. He places a hand on my shoulder. "Let us help. Please."

I step aside, and the Zmaj step forward, pushing the boys aside. One of them takes her head between his hands and leans close. He studies her face and presses his fingers along her neck while keeping her head still. At last he peels back her eyes, stares into them a moment, then looks up at us.

"She's not taking epis?" he asks.

"None of us do," I say.

"You don't?" Khabri asks, moving into my personal space.

I step back so I don't have to crane my neck to look up at him, and so I can breathe. When he's that close, it takes my breath away. He's dominant, screaming alpha maleness, even the scent of him is musky manliness.

"No," I say.

"Why would we? We're not going to be a slave to some drug," Petras says, inserting himself into the conversation.

"Humans need epis," Khabri says.

"Your bodies aren't evolved to survive on Tajss," Mageir says. "How have you made it this long without taking it?"

"We live underground," I say. "Is she going to be okay?"

"She's suffering extreme dehydration," Mageir says.

"So give her water," Liam says. "She doesn't need a drug."

"She does," Mageir says. "Water isn't going to be enough, not now. She's gone too far."

As if on command, she stops seizing and lies as still as death.

"Maeve!" I yell, pushing past Khabri. Her face is cold and clammy. She doesn't respond. I look at Mageir. "Help her!"

"She needs epis," he says, shaking his head. "I don't think anything else will save her."

The survivors of the mining settlement are huddled around the table where she's lying. I straighten and look at them.

"We have to save her," I say.

"She'd rather be dead than take that," Petras says.

"You're an idiot," Aurora says. "No one would rather be dead. Give it to her. Hell, I want some too. I'm tired of feeling like shit."

"Give it to her," I order when no one else speaks.

Mageir opens a small pouch at his waist and pulls out a piece of epis. It looks like a dried weed. He forces her mouth open, places it inside then moves her jaw to chew for her. Almost immediately her color is better. She doesn't wake up—it's not a miracle—but it's noticeably helping.

"She'll need rest, but she'll recover," Mageir says, stepping away from Maeve.

The mining colonists gather around and lift her up together without a word. Morgana leads as they take her away, leaving me alone with the Zmaj. Worse, alone with Khabri.

Great.

"Thanks," I say.

"Mageir is skilled in medicines and has knowledge of human biology," Khabri says.

As if on some unspoken cue, the other Zmaj disperse around the room leaving me well and truly alone with him. Wonderful. This is getting better and better.

"I'm glad he was here to help," I say, looking towards the door my friends left through.

"I am too," he says.

The worst part of all this is I like him. He's a nice guy, strong, really easy on the eyes, if you ignore the scales, horns, tail, and wings. Though they do add to his silhouette.

I've always liked big men, which leads me to wonder why the hell I ever thought Phillip would work out. He's anything but a big guy. And... here's Khabri, waiting for me to carry my half of the conversation. Great, this is awkward.

"Well, guess I should go too," I say, turning away.

As soon as my back is to him, I feel the weight of his gaze on my ass. As I take a step away, my butt warms, and I'm certain he's undressing me with his eyes. My cheeks flush, but whether it's because he's doing it, or because of how much I like it, I'm not sure.

"You need epis as well," he says.

I stop and turn around slowly. "Excuse me?"

"You need epis," he says again.

"I only agreed to give it to her because she was seizing. I'm fine," I say, pressing my fingers against my temples to keep my head from blasting apart.

"You are not," he says, closing the distance between us. "You must take care of yourself. You need epis."

The hackles on the back of my neck stand on end. "And who do you think you are to order me around?"

"I am your mate," he says, full of swagger and confidence. "I will care for you, no matter what."

"I can take care of myself fine," I snap, glaring through the pain in my head.

"Yes," he agrees. "I apologize if I implied otherwise. It is not your ability for self-care. You are a strong female. One of the strongest I have ever met. You are also the most beautiful on this planet."

My cheeks are red hot, and it takes all my will to keep my glare and not melt into his arms. Who in the hell says things like that?

"It will be my honor, my privilege, and my duty to care for you in all ways. Your every desire will be my command. You will it, I will make it happen. You shall want for nothing."

"You're..." I trail off.

It's impossible to think. He's so damn close. The scent of

him is heady, conjuring images of twisted sheets and long, sweaty nights filled with pleasure.

"Yours," he says, filling in the empty blank I left hanging.

My heart leaps into my throat. I shake my head no even as I take an involuntary step closer, drawn in by the force of him. He's so... here.

Big. Strong. Certain of himself, and certain about me even if I'm not. He risked his life to save not only mine, but all my friends. He hasn't asked for a thing in return, and here I am being a bitch.

But he's a Zmaj. Alien.

I never fully bought into Gershom's shit, but the Zmaj *are* scary. He's scary, or he can be. The force he displayed fighting to save all of us was terrifying. I stop moving closer, but the air is electric. My fingers tingle with my desire to touch him. What do his scales feel like?

I've never touched a Zmaj. Drosdan is the only one who ever came around the mining colony, and he was Sarah's. Are the scales hard? Or flexible? Are they cold?

The tiny scales covering his face stop above the flesh of his lips. I can't tear my eyes away. Acting on impulse, I kiss him.

It's fast, almost too fast to say I did it, except sparks snap between us as our lips brush against each other, and the warmth in my belly ignites into a raging fire. His arms move towards an embrace, but he stops when I break the kiss. I watch the tiny movements of his eyes, savoring the taste of his lips.

Neither of us blinks or breathes. The moment stretches.

CRASH! The moment breaks as both of us jerk towards the noise.

"I've got it," Amara says, gathering up the dishes she spilled.

"Sorry," I mumble, touching my lips and not looking back at him. "I shouldn't have done that."

His brow furrows. It looks like he's vibrating with desire. An urge to kiss him again, more fully, pushes into my thoughts, but I stop myself, this time.

"Please, let me get you epis," he says after a long moment. "You need it."

I close my eyes and try to find my footing. I can't believe I did this. I'm so stupid. Now he's talking, and I'm spinning in my head while my body is aching. My head hurts so bad I want to cry, and my stomach flips between burgeoning desire and nauseated mess.

"I'm sure there's not enough," I whisper, looking around the dining hall.

The few people that are eating on this shift stare listlessly at their underfilled plates. We don't have enough food. How could there be enough epis? It's hard to store, and there was always a shortage of it before the siege.

Khabri reaches towards me then stops before he touches my shoulder, pulling his hand back to his side. I watch his face and there's no harmful intent, even if he is being insistent. He purses his lips, which taste like peaches, then shakes his head.

"Anna." The way he says my name, there's a weight to it as if he somehow gives it gravity. "I will take care of you. Always. Please let me."

Ah, damn it. My heart is racing, and my knees are weak. How can he keep saying things that make me feel like this? I'm a fool. I know it. An obstinate, stupid fool. What other man would ever offer what he wants to give freely?

Not a one. I know it. So what's the stop?

"I... can't," I say. It comes out as a whisper, not because I mean it to, but I can't muster the strength to speak louder. He leans closer, distracting.

"Why not?" he asks.

117

"They need it more," I say.

The honesty of my words tears at my soul as I speak. I'm naked before him. I let my shields down as I put my trust into another person for the first time I can remember. No guarding, no holding back, nothing hidden.

I plead with my eyes, begging for him to understand.

13

KHABRI

"They need it more," she whispers.

My hearts shatter and my breath catches in my throat.

"I will get it," I say, forcing words past the lump in my throat.

She shakes her head, her eyes glistening as moisture forms in their corners. She blinks rapidly then inhales deeply.

"I'm fine," she insists.

My arms ache with emptiness. Nothing would make me happier than to hold her. Shield her from this world. I'm pulled into her, unable to escape the vortex of my feelings.

"Anna," I say. "Your heart is admirable. This is not our end. I know it. Please, trust in me if you can't trust fate. Trust me."

Her lips tremble. A single drop of moisture trails down her cheek. She swipes her arm across her face, then nods. I hold out my hand, and when she takes it my hearts race. I lead the way to the stock supplies of the city. The male known as Bert is waiting with his arms crossed and a scowl on his face.

"We don't have any," he snaps as soon as we enter the room.

"I have not asked for anything yet," I say.

"Don't matter, we don't have it," he says.

Red tinges my vision at his surliness. I straighten to my full height, towering over the much smaller male and partially open my wings.

"She needs epis," I say, lowering my voice.

Bert pales but doesn't back down. He tightens his jaw and narrows his eyes.

"We especially don't have enough of *that*," he says.

The bijass swells leaving me awash in anger bordering on blind rage. I growl and struggle to control the primal instinct.

"Bert," Anna says. "I'm sorry. I know there's not enough, I'll…"

She trails off, grabbing her head and whimpering with obvious pain.

"Ah damn it," Bert swears, pushing past me and taking her by her arms.

He guides her to a chair, then rushes to a counter and gets a container of water. He holds it up to her lips and helps her to sip it.

It jerks me to my senses. This is not an adversary, no matter he is blocking me. It has been most of a lifetime since I've felt the pull of the bijass so strongly. It must be the conflict of my desire to protect her strengthening primal urges. I'll have to be more careful to stay in control.

"You all right?" Bert asks her.

"Sorry, yes," she says, sipping more water.

"She is suffering dehydration," I say. "Please, I need epis for her."

Bert looks over his shoulder to me, a deep frown on his face. He shakes his head, sighs heavily, then stands up. He still has one hand on her shoulder, making slow circles.

I am jealous, but it is easily controlled. There is no sexual intent in his touch, so it does not spark the bijass. My jealousy is only in her letting him touch her when all I want is to touch her.

I want to feel her skin. In my imagination it is soft and delicate, as her lips were when she kissed me. I have never touched a human's skin. Their distinct lack of scales is exotic, and I dream of getting to know every inch of her.

Bert walks past me to a door at the back of the room.

"In here," he says.

I follow him through the door. He walks down the rows of shelves, most of which are distressingly barren. At the end of the row he turns left and goes down to a wall. There he opens a cabinet and pulls out a folded piece of tanned leather. He carefully unfolds the package to reveal strands of epis.

He breaks off a piece then conscientiously folds the leather back up the way it was. He places the package in its place, shuts the door, and turns around with the strand held out in his open palm. I take it from him but don't turn to leave. I stare at the cabinet where he retrieved the epis.

"What?" he asks.

"Is that all the supplies you have?" I ask.

Bert looks over his shoulder at the cabinet before answering.

"Yes," he exhales heavily. The admission deflates him. His shoulders slump, and his chin drop to his chest. "God help us, yes."

I turn to leave but stop again and study the storage space. This is all the supplies the City has left. It isn't enough for more than a week at most and the epis supply looks like it won't make it that long. I walk along the shelves, taking a mental inventory. I understand his surliness now.

In a few days, the true weight of the Invaders' siege will be felt. If we don't do something soon, there won't be any fight left for us. We must find a way to get supplies into the city.

I lead the way back to Anna. She is still sitting in the chair, bent over and holding her head in her hands. I kneel before her and hold out my palm. She sits up. Her face is too pale, and beads of sweat have formed all across it. Her hand shakes as she reaches for the epis.

"You're sure?" she asks, voice trembling.

"Yes, my trea—" I cut myself off when she starts to pull her hand back. "Yes."

She looks up to meet my eyes and shakes her head.

"Can we… keep it slow?" she asks. My heart leaps into my throat. My mouth is too dry for words, so I nod. She takes the epis and holds it up before her face, considering it. "So little, for such a life-changing thing."

She places it in her mouth and chews. Her eyes widen, then color rushes back into her face. She shivers then straightens.

"Wow," she says.

"Better?" I ask.

"Yeah," she says, still chewing. "It's weird, kind of spicy but sweet. Tangy."

She stands up and wavers. I grab her arm to steady her without thinking. Our eyes meet and my hearts gallop. I'm pulled in. I can't resist her. I've stood against every danger Tajss has to offer and nothing compares to her. I will do anything for her. This simple touch is all I could ever ask in return.

She drops her gaze to my hand then looks back and forth from my face and my touch. I should let her go, but I can't. Can't break this simple contact. Can't not touch her.

She leans towards me, taking a step until less than the width of my hand separates us. I'm hunched down, close to her face. Her scent is intoxicating. I'm spinning in a whirlpool of her. I move in, wanting to taste her. She doesn't retreat, lifting herself on her toes. So close—

"Are you two about done with the puppy-dog eyes?" Bert asks, breaking the moment.

She drops onto her feet and I straighten, feeling oddly self-conscious.

"Yes," I say, turning to him. "Thank you for your help."

"Right, move on then. Some of us have work to do," he says.

Anna walks ahead, and I follow in her wake. Outside the building she stops, holding her hands up and turning them back and forth. A smile forms on her face that is more brilliant than the double suns of Tajss.

"Wow," she says.

"Yes?" I ask.

"I feel… better," she says, wonder in her voice. "A lot better, already."

"Epis is Tajss's gift of life," I say.

"That sounds like some mystical bivo-shit to me," she says. "But I do feel so much better. I think I could leap that big fountain!"

"How about we wait for heroics?" I ask, smiling, and she laughs.

The sound of her laugh makes my heart sing. My chest swells with love and pride. There is nothing I won't do to hear that sound over and over.

Behind my joy, though, are darker thoughts. The empty supply room hasn't left my mind since seeing those bare shelves. She will need more epis. Since this is the first time she's taken it, she'll need more in the next few days at the most. Ideally, she'd take it every day for weeks until it's had time to fully work its way through her body.

She feels great now, I'm sure, but tomorrow that will be gone. The day after that she'll feel the first hints of withdrawal. There is going to be no time to waste on getting her more. All of them need it.

"Why did I wait so long to take this?" she says, laughing and shaking her head.

She whirls in a circle, holding her arms out to either side as she does. When she stops, she's staring at me thoughtfully. She closes the distance between us. In an instant, she throws her arms around my neck, pulls my head down, and kisses me.

This is not a quick peck. Her lips press hard against mine, and liquid fire races through my veins. My core tightens, and my prime cock stiffens as I give myself to her. Her tongue licks my lips then pushes into my mouth. I lick her tongue, too.

She breaks the kiss and steps back. She touches her lips, still smiling. I wait, apprehensive, until she laughs long and loud.

"Wow," she says. "You are a really good kisser."

"Thank you," I say, standing straighter.

"Can I touch your chest?" she asks. It's such an odd request I don't answer for a heartbeat, but then I nod my assent. She traces her fingers over my pectoral muscles. "They're so smooth."

"What did you expect?" I ask.

She shakes her head. "I don't know."

She continues running her fingertips over my chest, and then she places both palms on back on the same scales and rubs small circles. Desire is a raging inferno in my core. My cock throbs, expelling the first droplets of my seed.

She giggles and pulls her hands back. My body is as taut as a drum skin, still vibrating from her touch. The dragon roars to take her, to keep this going, to bring her closer. It's all my will to resist, despite my years of training. I've never been tested the way she tests me. Being so close, having dreamed of her for years now, I know we belong together. It is a foregone conclusion, but she is not ready. I will not diminish our love by rushing her.

I have waited this long, but that doesn't matter. It is still the hardest thing I've ever done.

"I need to see Rosalind," I say.

My voice is rough, almost guttural, for my throat is so swollen with unexpressed desire. She tilts her head, not missing the difference, and nods.

"Let's go," she says, offering me her hand.

I take her hand in mine. Hers is tiny, delicate and soft. I cup my hand around hers, careful to not apply pressure. As we walk to find Rosalind, my steps become lighter. I'm walking on the clouds.

There aren't many people on the streets. Almost everyone is staying in the tunnels under the city, despite the bombing having stopped. They feel safer, though I know it won't make a difference if the dome comes down. Nor will it save them from the impending disaster of food and epis running out.

We run into no one we know before reaching the city offices where Rosalind works. She looks up as we walk in, but she's not alone. Visidion, Ladon, and Sverre are with her, as are Calista and Amara.

"Yes?" Rosalind asks.

"I've come to offer the Order's assistance in getting supplies into the City," I say.

"You have a bright idea how to do it?" she snaps.

Rosalind looks drawn. The lines at the corners of her eyes are deeper, her mouth is turned down in a frown, and there are heavy bags under her eyes. I don't answer her, though. Weariness and stress don't excuse rude behavior. I've found that many times silence can be the strongest rebuke.

The silence stretches, but Rosalind has her attention on the papers on her desk, ignoring me. The others in the room shift uncomfortably while I wait silently.

"Hey, we want to help," Anna says. "If you got this on your own, you don't have to be a bitch."

Rosalind's head snaps up, eyes glaring. I take a step forward subtly putting myself partially in front of Anna.

"Excuse me?" Rosalind asks.

"I said—" Anna starts.

"I am here to offer help," I say, sorry to cut Anna off. "I have able males who will fight as needed. There must be a way out of the city. I know the supplies are already running low. I don't see how there is time to fight with each other when the enemy is at our gates."

Visidion places a hand on Rosalind's shoulder, easing her back into her chair.

"Your offer is appreciated," Visidion says. "We will be needing males."

"Do you have a plan?" I ask.

I haven't missed that the papers covering her desk are maps and some look like blueprints.

"Some of those tunnels under the city lead beyond the dome," Amara says. "We're trying to figure out which one we might be able to use to sneak a group out. Make a run for the Tribe. Get help and supplies too."

"A sensible plan," I say. "I will join the group going."

Rosalind and Visidion exchange a look, and then she nods almost imperceptibly. Visidion looks at Ladon. Ladon looks me up and down.

"I've seen you fight," he says. "Fine. I'll bring you."

"You're not leading this," Calista says.

Ladon looks away to his mate. "Calista, you know I must."

"No," she says, her face pale, tears on her cheeks. "Someone else can be the hero this time. You've done enough." She rushes across the room to him, cupping his face in her hands. "How many times are you going to do this to me? Please, stay home. We need you."

"My love," he says, shaking his head. "I must protect you and our son. What kind of mate would I be if I don't do this?"

"Ladon," she pleads. "Please. I've got a really bad feeling about this."

"Calista, I would do anything for you. You know—"

"Then stay!"

"You are my treasure. My sacred duty. And as such, I am bound to care for you. I must do this."

Her mouth opens to protest, but she snaps it shut and turns away from him. Anna is staring at the two of them, wide-eyed but thoughtful. I do not envy Ladon. He feels he is duty bound, which I understand he is. He must protect his mate and his children.

This is the first time I'm glad I didn't find Anna long before now. If we had children already, I don't know how I would keep myself focused. The others may not see it, but I feel Ladon's pain. It's tearing his soul apart, but he is doing what he must.

"Here," Amara says, pointing at the map on Rosalind's desk. "This tunnel is the one I remember. It goes past the dome and opens two dunes out on the east. We can make our way to the Tribe from there."

"Fine, let's go," Ladon says without hesitation.

"I'm going, too," Anna says.

"No," I say.

"You're not the boss of me," she says, stepping back, hands on her hips.

"This will be dangerous," I say.

"And staying here is safe?"

"Anna, I will not take you outside the dome. Stay here. We'll return shortly."

"Like hell you're going to tell me what to do," she says. "I can fight, but did you forget that I'm a miner? I know tunnels. Can any of you say the same?"

Amara raises her hand. "I know the tunnels pretty well."

"Pretty well compared to? Are you sure the tunnels beyond the dome are safe? Do you know how to check them for faults and other dangers? No? I didn't think so." She whirls around to me. "See? You need me."

"I don't see—" I say.

"She's right," Rosalind says, cutting me off. "We don't know what shape the tunnels are in. Beyond the shield the bombings could have done a lot more damage. I can't lose my team out there to something stupid we could have prevented."

Calista is looking at me and understanding passes between us. She pleads with her eyes, and I wish I could reassure her. I can't. I'm as worried as she is.

I've got a bad feeling too.

14

ANNA

LADON LEADS OUR GROUP, PUSHING PAST THE PEOPLE congregated in the tunnels. Watching Ladon reminds me why I went with Gershom. He's not exactly mean, but he's indifferent. He barks at anyone who doesn't move out of his way fast enough. He growls if they ask questions. He makes my belly flutter, so that I want to recoil or run away. Yet here I am, following him.

If Khabri's right and there is some grand design, a manipulating hand of fate, then I must have royally pissed it off at some point in my life. I shouldn't have stolen that necklace from the shop when I was a kid. Maybe if I had been nicer to my mom?

I catalog my list of sins but honestly, I can't think of anything that left me deserving of all the shit that has happened. Certainly none that make it so I should be stuck in these narrow tunnels with an angry Zmaj.

Khabri is right behind me, bringing up the rear of our small group. Amara is right behind Ladon, guiding us, Shidan is behind her, and I'm following Sverre, who is behind Shidan. Two humans, four Zmaj.

Two boys for every girl! Dear god, I'm insane.

"We need to go left at the next intersection," Amara says, rattling the map in her hands as she refolds the paper to study a different part. "After that, we'll be at the entrance. There's a massive door, pain in the ass to unlock. We will be right at the edge of the dome then."

"Move," Ladon growls when a man doesn't get out of his way fast enough.

"Who are you," the guy complains.

Ladon grabs his shoulder and forces him to the side.

"Hey!" I exclaim.

Ladon looks over his shoulder and glares at me. My stomach ties itself into a knot while chills race down my spine. That came out of my mouth before I thought it through.

"We must hurry," Ladon says, his voice so low it sounds like a hiss.

I should keep my mouth shut. Say nothing, back down. Nod and let it go.

I should but….

"That doesn't mean you get to be a dick," I say instead.

My cheeks warm and my knees are shaking, but I've gone too far to back down. Ladon's eyes narrow, and the tip of his tail rises above his head. He turns around to look at me full on.

Oh, shit.

Khabri steps around in front of me and confronts Ladon head on. The two men glare at each other. The tension in the air is so great there's pressure on my skin. My heart thunders in my ears, leaving me counting the beats. One. Two. Still staring. Three. Four. Ladon leans forward, his hands curling into fists. Five. Six. This is bad.

"Enough," Sverre says. Shidan has an arm around Amara, shielding her from the coming conflict, but Sverre moves between the two men and holds an arm out towards each of them, palms out. "We do not have time for this. Control yourselves."

Ladon unclenches his fist, and his tail drops. The tension is gone that fast. He gives a half nod, turns around, and resumes walking as if nothing happened. I inhale loudly, the first breath I've dared to take since this began.

Khabri turns around, grips my shoulders firmly, and crouches down so he's eye to eye with me.

"Are you okay?" he asks.

"Yeah," I say, trying really hard to not shake.

"That was very brave," he says softly. "Admirable."

"Thanks," I say.

He smiles, holding my shoulders for a moment before he steps back into his position at the rear. I exhale heavily then rush to catch up to the others. Amara is right, it isn't far before we come to a massive door.

On the ship there were doors that led to high-pressure areas. When I was a kid playing hide-and-seek, I discovered a mainte- nance tunnel that let out on one. This door reminds me of that one. Thick-looking steel with reinforcing beams running across its surface. A massive wheel that looks bigger than me even now in the middle. The wheel has handles around its outside. It's obviously not meant for easy passage.

"Here we are," Amara says. "Shidan?"

Shidan walks up to the wheel. I half-expected it to look smaller with perspective, with the massive Zmaj next to it, but nope. It still looks huge. Shidan stretches his arms out fully to reach either side of the wheel. He strains to turn it.

Every muscle on his overly toned body tenses, bulging out, making it clear how incredibly strong their entire race is. Shidan isn't even that big, for a Zmaj.

Shidan grunts, then groans and tries again. The wheel doesn't budge. He lets go, steps back, and shakes his head.

Sverre has a big smile on his face. He places a hand on Shidan's shoulder then the two of them walk up to the wheel.

Together they lean into it and still they strain, but it moves with a soft screech. Once it starts moving, it loosens, and in a couple of minutes the door stands open.

A musty smell wafts out. Beyond the door, lies a roughhewn, unfinished tunnel with flickering lights set along the top of the wall every forty feet or so. There are cracks along the walls and some on the ceiling too. Large support beams that look like they are made of concrete are evenly spaced as far as I can see. Some of those also have cracks in them.

Amara looks to me. "Looks like you're up, miner girl."

She smiles and makes a sweeping motion forward with her hand.

"Thanks." I smile and walk up to the mine.

Khabri follows. I walk into the tunnel and up to the first of the cracks on the wall. After running my hands up and down the wall, I press around the split, testing how the wall reacts. It seems to be holding well enough.

Satisfied with that first test, I go to the beam that has a long crack running up and down it. This is the one I'm most worried about. When I press, there's a soft crack and fresh dirt drizzles out of it.

"This isn't safe," I say. "But it will hold for now. If they bomb us again, I don't think this tunnel will hold up."

"Then we need to hurry," Ladon says.

He moves past, his wings pushing me up against the wall. I bite my tongue before I spout off at the mouth again. Khabri stops to make sure I'm okay. I nod and take my place in our group. We walk on in silence.

I'm continuously studying the walls and ceiling, but I've done this for so long now that it's automatic, leaving me with way too much time to think.

Ladon is the epitome of why I was scared of the Zmaj. I followed Gershom not because I believed him, but because what was the alternative? Stay in the City with Ladon and the other new Zmaj showing up? No thanks.

Khabri is different. He's proven that over and over, even if he is weirdly pushy. I can't imagine any human guy coming up and saying, hey, we're going to make great babies as an opening line. I mean, seriously?

He's sexy. He's protective, and he's a skilled warrior, a great trait to make sure you survive on Tajss. Yet I can't open up to him.

I want to, but every time I almost do, I stop myself. I like big guys. Every fantasy I've ever had is a big guy. What could it hurt to try?

Ladon reminds me why. Big guys also have tendencies to be demanding, intrusive, and to not care about those around them. Maybe Ladon's different with Calista, but what I've seen doesn't make me think so.

She was scared of him coming on this trip. She begged him not to go, but he's all, oh no, I'm the big strong man. I do what I want. A typical big guy trait. Is Khabri like that too? He hasn't been, at least that I've seen.

Shidan obviously dotes on Amara. Even walking through the tunnel, his eyes never leave her. He worships the ground she walks on. She seems to feel the same. They get along great.

Watching them makes me wonder what it would be like to have someone like that. Khabri wants to be. All I have to do is say yes. Say yes to an alien-dragon man who, if rumors are true, has a double down on alien monster dong. Heat forms in my belly thinking about it. There are a lot of half-Zmaj babies running around, so obviously it fits. I can't help but wonder what that would be like.

I can't deny it'd be nice to be able to get off myself every time. Two cocks ought to mean one for his pleasure, one for mine, right?

Something cracks. Dirt falls from the ceiling.

"Run!" I yell.

Everyone rushes ahead. Another crack echoes off the walls, and more dirt falls. No one stops, but I watch over my shoulder praying we're not about to have a cave-in. Luckily, it stops before any more damage happens.

"Okay," I say. "We're okay."

"You scared the hell out of me," Amara says, wiping sweat from her forehead.

"Better safe than sorry," I say.

"I'm not complaining, observing only," she says, holding up her hand.

"We're here," Ladon says, pointing ahead to where the tunnel dead ends and a ladder is built into the wall.

He doesn't wait for anyone before climbing the ladder. There's a much smaller door that's a mini version of the previous one at the top. Ladon spins this wheel easily and then lifts the door a crack. Sand blows in the small opening as he stares out.

None of us dare breathe, afraid even the noise of our breath might alert Invaders, if any are waiting. Ladon grunts and pushes the door open the entire way, and then he climbs out. There's no sounds of battle happening, so the rest of us scramble up and out.

We emerge on the open desert with both suns beating down. The heat is oppressive, but not as bad as it was before I took epis. Interesting.

After Khabri is out, Ladon closes the door and brushes sand back across to conceal its location. Behind us, I see the top of the dome of the city peeking over the summits of massive sand dunes that lie between it and us.

"This way," Ladon says, and he takes off across the desert.

Amara rolls her eyes before she jogs after him. Khabri waits for me to run, and then he paces me. I don't know if I can keep the pace Ladon is setting, but I'll try. We're only minutes into the running before I'm feeling how hard this is going to be.

At least there isn't time to let my thoughts wander. It's taking all my concentration to keep pushing myself to keep up.

We run for maybe an hour when I finally stumble to a stop. Amara stops, too. Ladon runs on for several feet before stopping and looking back with clear irritation. He doesn't say anything, but he does walk back to where we've stopped.

"I could carry you," Shidan offers Amara.

"It'll be a cold day on Tajss before I let you do that," Amara says. "I'm not weak."

"Of course not, my treasure," Shidan says.

"I can, if you'd like," Khabri offers. I give him an arched eyebrow and tilt of my head. He smiles and shakes his head. "Of course not."

Smart boy. I could get to like you.

Oh hell, I do like him. Damn it. He's sweet, attentive, and everything I could ever ask for in a man. Except for the whole let's make babies right now thing. That's still creepy.

I drink some water and Amara does the same. This is much easier with my one dose of epis, but it's still not a walk in the park. I know from experience, though—if I hadn't taken the epis I'd be throwing up, or on the ground in a ball praying to die.

"We can go," I say.

Ladon takes one step forward, then stops. He turns his head back towards us, his eyes narrowing.

"Down!" he hisses.

"Huh?" I ask, but then Khabri pulls me down to the ground.

He pushes until I'm flat on my belly next to him.

"Hide them," Ladon whispers. "They're too close."

I don't know what he's talking about, but my heart races as adrenaline pours out.

"Please forgive me," Khabri whispers, and I yelp in surprise as he rolls on top of me.

His weight pushes me down into the sand. Then he does some kind of shifting with his tail and wings, and it pushes us both deeper into the sand. Now my heart is pounding for a different reason.

I can't open my mouth to scream, because if I do, sand will pour in. In moments I'm deep in a hole in the sand with him on top of me. Above, there is a small crack of red sky and light.

Then I hear them.

Guttural grunts and clicks that can only be Invaders. Sand drizzles in through the small crack as the sound of their boots draws closer.

How Ladon heard this patrol coming I'll never know, but if he hadn't, we'd be fighting for our lives.

I close my eyes to keep the bits of sand out of them. I strain my hearing to the sounds of them coming closer. I'm so tense I feel stiff as a board. My imagination is running wild with possibilities. Visions of the six of us fighting our way out of here mix with us being captured. None of the possibilities are good.

The sound of their boots recedes, and we wait. Time passes strangely when you're buried beneath a large, well-muscled half-man, half-dragon. I don't know how long we've been waiting, but it's been a while.

And it's about now I become acutely aware of my ass and deciding that Khabri really is happy to see me, at least based on what's pressing hard against my butt.

It is big. It feels really big.

Now my imaginings are entirely different and, I'll admit, a hell of a lot better than what they were. This is probably stupid, but acting on a whim, I wriggle. Not a lot! Just shifting for a better position, that's all.

Khabri groans very softly in my ear.

It's the hottest, sexiest thing I've ever experienced. His hot breath passing over my cheek, his chest rumbling as the sound slips out. His cock pressing harder between my butt cheeks. I want him.

My timing couldn't be better, but the danger only makes it hotter. Makes me want him more. Lying here in this hole, shifting from thoughts of being captured and killed to having sex, the idea of having kids doesn't seem so bad. It would be nice, good even. A future generation, something to fight for and to give my life meaning.

Of course I've gone insane. Chemicals in my brain making me think like this. That's all it is. Chemical reaction, boy meets girl, body reacts. Biological clock or something.

Still... I can almost see a little girl in my mind's eye. Tiny, translucent wings and nubby little horns poking through her hair. Tiny, perfect fingernails.

Khabri rises out of the sand, pulling me up with him, cutting short my fantasy. Which is fine, better even. Now is not the time for fantasy.

"We need to move," Ladon says, softly. "They're still around."

No one needs to speak further. We resume the journey, and the suns are dropping low. Long shadows stretch across the sand like dark fingers stretching to capture us. As we make our way across the desert, the remnants of my fantasies dance at the edge of my thoughts, not quite going away.

What if?

15

ANNA

I'VE NEVER BEEN TO THE TRIBE'S CAVES BEFORE, BUT I'VE heard a lot about them. It's been clear for a while that Ladon was leading us towards a large outcropping that rises out of the sand ahead, but as we get closer and I can see the details, it's obvious this is a home.

The outcropping forms a C shape, curving out and around like a bay in a sea of desert. Closing in the bay thus formed is a curved wall. Or what remains of a wall. As soon as we see it Amara comes to a halt.

"Oh no," Amara mutters.

"There may be survivors," Shidan says. "We have to go and see."

The wall isn't a wall anymore. Jagged stones rising no more than a few feet are all that remain. Drosdan and Sarah lived here, and so many others. My stomach rebels, forcing bile up my throat, and I turn away.

"Are you okay?" Khabri asks.

"No," I say, fighting my stomach's intention of losing what little food it has.

I shake my head and sweat runs into my eyes. I'm light-headed, shaking, and my knees are weak. Khabri grips my shoulders. I shouldn't encourage him. I don't want to tease him, but right now, more than ever, I need someone to lean on.

I wrap my arms around him, and tears stream down my face. The images of what happened at the mining colony drift across my closed eyes. I squeeze him tighter. He wraps his arms around me. They're big, strong, and stable.

"Ahem," Amara clears her throat, jerking me out of my wallowing self-pity.

I rub my face with both hands before turning to face them. The three Zmaj with Amara stand silent, and even she has her eyes down.

"I'm sorry," she says, "but we need to move."

I nod my agreement. The lump in my throat blocks any words I could say. We resume walking, but no one is moving fast. I have chills like the light brushes of fingertips across my skin. It makes me shudder more than once.

My footsteps grow heavier, the closer we come. The destruction comes into focus, and then I can't tear my eyes away. Shattered stones dot the landscape. Once these were carefully shaped stones must have formed the wall I've been told about. A safe haven for the Tribe.

Now it's debris. Destroyed as if some god happened by and was displeased by their work. Smashing their wall with a giant fist.

Finally, I grow numb. Cool, cold, welcome numbness. My wished-for shield from the horror. As the shield falls into place, all this shock and distress becomes less impactful. As if it's not happening to me.

We stop at massive pieces of metal that once were probably gates. The two thick pieces are twisted like corkscrews lying on the ground. I close my eyes and offer a prayer to the universe that we find survivors. Part of me wishes I believed. I can see how comforting it would be to believe in fate. I'd welcome a certainty of my own survival.

My emotional armor cracks when we're inside the remnants of the wall. I was prepared for horrors, but that's not what I see. There are no bodies. No people besides ourselves. Nothing so dramatic breaches my protective shielding.

This *is* a home. Or it was.

Inside this wall, there is a wide-open area. To my right is an open area of hard-packed sand that looks like a playing field. Ahead of me grows a vibrant garden. A garden!

I can imagine Sarah and others working this beautiful field of lush greens and yellows. Hints of orange and some reds lined out in neat rows. Tools lie dropped as if they were in the middle of working when they abandoned them.

But no people. No bodies.

To the right, along the natural wall of the outcropping, are lean-to stations with worktables at their front and various tools behind the divide those tables form. My eyes are drawn to what looks like a forge. A massive hammer and a set of iron-looking tongs lie haphazardly next to cooling coals of the fire. Someone was working there when something happened.

"Where are they?" Amara mutters.

She walks off at an angle, aiming between the garden and the workshops. I follow along, as do the others. The garden comes out of a massive cavern that dives into the cliff face. The cliff face itself has a walkway cut into it. The path cuts back and forth, working its way up the face of the cliff in a series of Z shapes making four different levels. Dotting along each different level of the path are openings covered by pieces of thick leather.

Homes. That is where they slept.

Moving past the garden and closer to the yawning cavern we come to a flat area with long tables that have benches set on either side. It's close to the mouth of the cave and looks like a communal dining table.

An object lying in the dirt catches my eye. I kneel to pick it up gently. My heart shatters, bursting through my emotional shields. Tears stream down my face.

It's a doll. The body is handmade from mismatched pieces of cloth. It has black yarn hair sewn to its head, buttons for eyes, one of which is missing. Pieces of leather have been cut into the shape of wings and sewn to its back. A carved stick serves as a tail. It's a hybrid doll: half-human, half-Zmaj.

I clutch it to my chest, hunching over it, and cry. Khabri kneels beside me and slowly places his arm over my shoulders. Once more I find myself leaning on him. In his arms, I feel a measure of safety that I desperately need.

It takes me a few minutes to pull myself together. Crying isn't going to help the owner of this doll or anyone else. If they're counting on me, then I'm not going to let them down. We haven't found any bodies, so there is still hope.

Khabri and I rise to our feet. The others have moved on into the cave. I walk fast to catch up.

"Any signs?" I ask.

"Nothing," Amara says.

Ladon stalks around the area with hunched shoulders, studying every inch of the space. There's a kitchen setup including cooking fires and prep tables in here. Our communal meals at the mining colony were much smaller than this setup. Sarah said there were a lot of people living at the Tribe. I'd even thought about coming for a visit here. Now I wish I had.

"They left," Ladon pronounces.

The way he says it, as if we can't all see that, raises my hackles.

"Thank you, Captain Obvious," I say. "Any clue where or when? If they left here, where would they go? They didn't make

141

it to the City, have they not had time? Are they lost in the desert?"

"I do not know," Ladon says, giving me a blank look as Amara snorts.

He is obviously missing my sarcasm. Do Zmaj understand sarcasm anyway?

"I like her," Amara says.

Shidan and Sverre are smiling, maybe they get it. Ladon sees their smiles and frowns then growls low in his throat before turning his back to me.

"There is nothing here," he says. "The epis is this way. Let's harvest what we can and go."

He walks deeper into the cave and fades into the darkness.

"You know we need some light, right?" Amara asks.

His barely visible form stops, and he turns around, marching back with clear annoyance.

He walks behind a table and pulls out a torch. Holding it up six inches from his face, he belches flame. The torch catches into a blazing light. He hands it to Sverre, then walks away without a word.

Amara and I share a look. She shakes her head, mouths the word *boys* at me, then walks after Shidan while Sverre leads the way with the torch.

The entrance to the cave is, well, cavernous. High ceilings and lots of open space, but it quickly narrows as we head for the rear. It isn't far at all before we're facing a rough wall with a large crack in it. While the crack is big, it doesn't look big enough for a Zmaj.

Ladon doesn't stop though. He turns sideways and forces himself into the opening. I hear the sounds of his flesh scraping on the rock walls, and it makes my skin crawl with empathetic sympathy.

Shidan forces his way in next, followed by Amara, then

Sverre, and it's up to me. It's not bad for me, but I'm a third the size of the smallest Zmaj. As we move on, the sides narrow even tighter, forcing me to turn sideways to get through.

I don't know how far in I am when suddenly the space is too tight. I close my eyes and focus on breathing. I *feel* the weight of the rock all around, pressing in. Immediately I'm hyper-ventilating.

I press my hands against the wall, trying to push it back. I need space. I need out of here.

"Anna, it is okay," Khabri says.

"Can't. Do. This," I say through gritted teeth. "Need out. Get me out!"

I turn and throw myself at him, trying to push past and get the hell out of this nightmare. He's too big. I can't fit past him.

"Anna," he says. His voice deep, commanding and resonating. He puts an arm over my shoulders and gently pulls me closer. His smell fills my senses. It's musky with a hint of exoticness to it. He's so… here. "I am here. I have you."

He does. He has me, and in this stupid moment of incomparable weakness I realize, this is the moment I fall in love with him.

All my doubts, reservations, and pull back are blasted away. Gone in between the beatings of my heart. He has protected me, and I *like* it. I want it. I want him to hold me, to wrap myself in his arms, and never leave.

I stop hyper-ventilating and take in two, shaky breaths, then my heart stops racing.

"I'm fine," I say, pulling my shit together. I stand up straight and take a step away from him then I stop and look up into his glistening eyes. "Thank you."

It comes out a whisper, not because of choice or design, but because the lump in my throat won't let more through. When he doesn't say anything but nods instead, the doors to my heart are thrown wide and I could fall into him. No pressure and no gloating.

"You okay?" Amara asks, her voice echoing off the stone.

"Yeah," I say. I bite my lip, then give him a smile and make my way after the others.

Ahead is a soft bluish glow. I emerge from the crack into another wide-open cavern, but this one looks anything but natural. The 'cavern' is more of a tunnel. A massive tunnel, but a tunnel, nevertheless. Hanging from the ceiling like stringy stalactites are strand after strand of epis.

I've never seen it unharvested. It's strangely beautiful. Ladon puts out the torch in the loose sand that covers the floor. My eyes are drawn to it, and then I realize it's not only sand we're standing in. When I look at my feet, my stomach flips.

"Shit," I gasp, moving from foot to foot, but there's nowhere to go. The floor is covered with it.

"You didn't know?" Amara asks, laughing.

"Know what?" I ask, horrified.

"Where epis grows," she says.

I stop my pointless dancing to glare. "Hello? Mining colonist here. I never took epis before yesterday."

"How did you survive?" she asks her eyes widening. "I figured all you guys were taking it by now."

"We lived underground," I say. "No need to poison ourselves with it."

"Still would've been hot," Amara says. "I couldn't have done it."

"Well, we do. Or we did," I say.

"Impressive," Amara says "Well, crash course in epis then. It only grows in tunnels left behind by a zemlja, but that's only one aspect of it. It has to be fertilized, which is where the sismis come in. They roost in these tunnels, though the proximity of the

Tribe has driven this clutch to a different home. Their dung is the fertilizer."

"So why doesn't it grow from the ground?" I ask, staring up at the glowing strands.

"Hell if I know," Amara says. "Ask Calista or Jolie, though I'll warn you, be prepared if you do."

"Be prepared?" I ask.

"Oh yeah, you'll be there for hours," she says. "Or until you poke your eardrums out with the nearest sharp object. They're botanists, also known as b-o-r-i-n-g!"

I laugh. "Right, thanks for the heads up. So how do we... never mind."

I stop my question when I see Ladon cup his hands and Shidan put his foot into the saddle he creates. Ladon's wings open part way as his muscles ripple and he lifts Shidan into the air. Shidan stretches as far as he can with a small knife held in one hand and cuts a strand off as high as he can reach.

The strand drops to the ground, its glow dimming the moment it's cut from its base. Sverre carefully gathers the strand, looping its length around his arm while Ladon and Shidan cut another one.

"How do I help?" I ask.

"We need to wrap the strands in these specially oiled leathers," Amara says as she unfolds a large piece of leather and lays it out on the ground.

Sverre and Amara work precisely together, handling the epis with extreme care. I stand next to Khabri, unsure what I can do to help, but I watch in case I need to do it myself or see something I can do to help. A low rumble shakes the cavern.

"What's that?" I ask, looking around as dust fills the air, drifting off the ceiling.

"I don't know," Khabri says, walking towards the crack we came in here from.

He stares through the opening while the others finish wrapping the second strand.

"This is enough for now," Ladon says.

"Get back!" Khabri yells, spinning on his heel towards us and running at me like a freight train bearing down.

Before I can speak, he hooks his arm around my stomach, lifts me off my feet, and we're running. It knocks my air out, he grabbed me so hard. I'm gasping, trying to catch my breath as he carries me over his shoulder. I see what we're running away from, and as air rushes into my lungs, I expel it in a scream.

The wall around the crack glows bright red-orange, then it explodes.

Shards of rock scream through the air, cutting my arms and face and burning the wounds closed as fast as they form. Khabri jerks me off his shoulder and shields me with his body. I smell the scent of burnt flesh, but he doesn't cry out or make a sound, running deeper into the tunnel.

Everyone is running ahead into the constant blackness. Behind us, Invaders were pouring through the opening they blasted in the wall. Now I hear their boots echoing off the walls. There's sunlight ahead. Khabri runs faster, seeing a possible escape.

The walls disappear as we emerge into a cavern. Above us is an opening to the red Tajss sky, but there's no way to reach it. This cavern isn't as tall as the original opening where the Tribe had their kitchens, but it's still too tall for even the Zmaj to reach up and pull us out.

Khabri sits me down as we all evaluate if we can make an escape or a stand. Pillars that are about as thick as me dot the open area, reaching from floor to ceiling. Invader boots storm down the tunnel, coming closer with each passing second.

"That tunnel is collapsed," Sverre says, pointing at the only other exit.

"I don't see a way out," Shidan says, pulling his lochaber off his back.

Ladon's wings flutter, then his tail rises up past his head, vibrating.

"Do as I say," he orders.

He moves to stand beneath the opening. "Shidan, come here."

He cups his hands nodding. Shidan follows the obvious solution, putting his foot into Ladon's hands. Ladon heaves Shidan skyward. Shidan opens his wings and gets his hands on the edge of the opening.

He's scrabbling, wings flapping, sand pouring in, then he finds purchase and crawls his way over the side. In a moment, he reappears in the opening, sticking his hand down. Ladon throws Amara up to him next. Shidan grabs her arm and pulls her out.

"Go," Khabri says. Grabbing me by my waist, he rushes to the opening, and not waiting for Ladon, throws me up into the air himself.

I yelp and wave my arms, but Shidan snatches me easily. He jerks me up and over, and I land with a thump on the desert sand.

Metal clangs on metal emerging from the crack in the ground. With my heart thundering, I race to the opening on my hands and knees and look in.

A dozen Invaders are engaged with the Zmaj. Khabri is fighting three of them and holding his own, but it's not going to be enough. There are too many of them.

"Sverre!" Ladon yells.

Sverre is fighting two Invaders, glances at Ladon, and nods. His lochaber whistles as it becomes a complete blur in the air, forcing the Invaders back as the spinning lochaber makes what looks like dozens of small cuts on each of them. The moment they back up, he turns and runs at Ladon.

He leaps towards Ladon, his foot extending and landing in

Ladon's waiting hands. Ladon heaves him up at the same moment as a club slams against Sverre's leg, and I hear something crack.

Sverre cries out, but Shidan catches his arm and pulls him out of the opening. Sverre crawls out of the way, dragging one leg behind him.

Khabri is hard pressed. There are too many Invaders. Ladon has engaged four of them, but they're forcing him back, away from the crack above. I'm too scared to scream. Frozen in place, watching these men fight for their lives. Fight for mine and all our lives.

Ladon is using one of the pillars to tangle the Invaders. Dodging from one side to the other. One of the Invaders fighting him roars and slams its club into the pillar. The pillar cracks and the ground I'm lying on rumbles.

A light shines in Ladon's eyes. I see it from here, like a lightbulb turned on.

"Come on!" Ladon yells, dancing around that pillar. "Come on!"

Two of the Invaders swing, but it's clear this is Ladon's plan. Their clubs slam against the pillar again, and this time Ladon turns and runs. The pillar implodes, dust rising up where it was, and then the ceiling collapses.

I can't leave. The opening is bigger now as the ground collapses. The four Invaders Ladon was fighting are buried in a ton of sand and rock. Ladon runs toward Khabri where he still fights, but Ladon has taken many small wounds, and blood is pouring down his chest, his face, and on his arms.

"Khabri!" Ladon yells.

He stoops as he runs, cupping his hands before him. Khabri glances, sees him coming, then attacks with an incredibly primal ferocity. He charges the Invaders, blade swinging in wild wide arcs. The Invaders fall back at his charge, and then he turns and runs for Ladon.

Shidan throws himself flat on the ground and reaches into the hole. Khabri flies up and Shidan catches his arm, pulling him over the edge. He scrambles around, lies flat next to Shidan.

"Ladon, leap!" Khabri barks.

Time slows to a crawl. The Invaders regroup and move towards Ladon, but Ladon looks as if he has nothing but time. He looks up at the three of us, and I join them yelling for him to jump. He shakes his head.

"Tell Calista and Illadon," he says. "I love them."

He turns to face the oncoming attackers.

"NO! Jump, we can catch you," Khabri yells.

"Fly, fools," Ladon says. He attacks the pillar with his lochaber.

The first blow rattles it, and the ground we're standing on rumbles.

"Ladon, no!" Shidan yells.

Ladon swings again. Before the shaft of his weapon connects, Khabri grabs me and runs. The ground rumbles loudly. Shidan leaps to his feet and gives us chase.

An instant later, the rumble becomes a roar. The ground for thirty feet around the crack collapses, and a massive cloud of dirt and sand explodes into the air, towering into the sky.

16

KHABRI

I WRAP MYSELF AROUND ANNA, ENCLOSING HER IN MY ARMS AND wings. Debris strikes my back as the cloud of dirt engulfs us. I lift her and run. I don't know if the ground will continue to give way, but it's too dangerous to stay here.

We emerge from the edge of the dirt cloud. Sverre and Shidan are right behind us, with Amara in Shidan's arms. Almost as one, we come to a stop and turn to look back. No one speaks, but my hearts thunder in my chest.

Ah, Ladon. An act of bravery that is incomparable. Statues should be erected in his honor. They won't be. There aren't enough survivors on the planet to have time for honoring those who've sacrificed themselves, not when our own survival is far from assured.

The dust hasn't fully settled before Amara runs forward but Shidan wisely grabs his mate and stops her. I set Anna down, but she stays close to my side. I wait four heartbeats, and then the dust has cleared enough to see.

The ground looks like a crater left after an impact. The cavern has collapsed and stretches from a wingspan in front of us clear to the cliff that is the back side of the Tribe's home.

Sverre walks forward, testing the footing before committing his weight. Sand slides into the pit, covering over the debris. I wait with bated breath, watching Sverre creep out to where we last saw Ladon.

There can be no doubt that he is lost to us. The destruction is great. He died to save all of us. Sverre reaches the approximate area where Ladon would have been, and he kneels. He throws stones aside and tries to dig down. The ground trembles, and the loose rock he's on shifts.

"Zemlja," Shidan says, staring across the desert. "Incoming, fast."

I look in the same direction Shidan is, and it's easily seen. The zemlja isn't hiding its progress. The desert sands plume along its path.

"Sverre, we must move," I say.

"I hear something," Sverre says, digging faster.

The ground rumbles again, and then the rocks shift beneath him and collapse further. He is dragged down with them. His wings spread, flapping at the wind, but his leg is stuck fast.

"Wait here," I order Anna, and I keep looking into her face until she nods agreement.

I spread my wings and bound across the debris. It shifts underfoot each time I land, but I move fast enough to not be caught. Sverre fights to free himself but the ground shifts more, and he's sinking deeper.

When I reach him, I grab his arm and pull. He growls. Sharp rocks cut through the protective scales of his leg. The rock I'm on slides aside, and I lose my footing, falling onto my back, knocking the breath out of me.

Sverre falls backwards when I do, and his body weight pulls his leg free. The debris is shifting more, vibrating with the approaching zemlja.

"Hurry!" Amara yells.

Sverre and I help each other across the shifting ground, working our way free of the trap. There's no time for mourning. The zemlja approaches, and we're in no condition to fight it. All of us have multiple wounds. Protecting the human females while fighting a zemlja is not going to work.

We do the only sensible thing. We run.

I grab Anna without asking. She would never be able to keep up, and we need to move. As a group we run around the sink-hole, cutting a wide berth, heading towards the Tribe's home. The rumbling of the ground grows louder. A few more bounds farther, and the ground is undulating.

We reach the cliff, skirting around its side and leaving the zemlja behind us. These large rock outcroppings will slow a zemlja down if nothing else. Once we reach the far side, we slow our pace, gathering as a group.

Anna looks back towards where we were. Tears stream down her face. Amara walks over and pulls her into an embrace. I exchange a look with the other males, and we all shift our weight awkwardly, giving them a few moments of grief.

"I can't believe this," Amara says.

"We should go back," Anna says. "He might have survived."

Sverre and I look at each other, both knowing that it's not possible, but neither of us want to be the one to say it. Sverre shrugs, and I know it's on me.

"Anna," I say, trying to make my voice like a hand to wipe her tears away. "It is not possible."

"He can't be gone!" Amara yells. "How am I supposed to face Calista if we don't try?"

"There is still too much danger," I say. "We need to move, get what epis we have, and get back to the City."

Amara shakes her head, but then she wipes her face with both hands, drying her tears. She takes Anna by her shoulders, pulling her around so they are face-to-face.

"Sometimes we lose good men," Amara says. "It happens, but he sacrificed himself to save us. We can't dishonor his memory by not doing what he wanted. Living. Going back at this point is stupid. There's not only the zemlja. That plume and eruption will attract Invaders."

Anna wipes her eyes with her sleeve and nods.

"Right," she murmurs.

I admire Amara and her determination. She has the soul of a warrior. Shidan beams with pride at his mate, and well he should. Still, there is no time to waste. We head off on our return to the City.

"Calista is going to be heartbroken," Anna says after we've walked for a long time.

"Yes," I say. "It is a terrible thing to lose your soul mate."

"I don't believe in soul mates," Anna says.

"How can you not?" I ask. "I knew, the moment I saw you, you're the one I was looking for. When I first heard you humans had come to Tajss, I knew my mate was among them. I knew it because I felt you in my soul."

"You were probably horny," Anna says. "How long has it been since you've been laid?"

"Few females survived the Devastation. Those who did grew sick and died," I say. "I do not understand your question."

She shakes her head. "Why are there no females? Is it really across the entire planet no females survived? Why?"

"I am not a physician, but I know generally why," I say. "Those of us who survived happened to be protected when the Devastation occurred. There were some females, at first. Even some children born afterwards."

"There were kids after the Devastation?" Anna asks, eyes wide.

The others have moved their way closer as I speak, listening in on my conversation. How much am I safe to say? I cannot reveal the Order secrets and a lot of what I'm talking about could, intentionally or not.

"There were," I say. "All males though."

"Why? And what happened to them?"

"The sex of a Zmaj baby is determined by the temperature at the time of conception, or so I've been told. Perhaps it is determined at some point in the gestation period. I do not honestly know when, but I do know it is affected by the temperature. When the Devastation happened, the temperature of Tajss soared."

"So only boys were born, the females died, and here we are," Anna says.

"And here we are," I agree.

"How did the females die?" she asks.

My stomach churns at the memory. The sickness that rotted them away was terrible, a second devastation in its own right.

"Radiation poisoning," I say.

"How come the males could handle it?" she asks.

"Most didn't. Those of us who survived, mostly, were immune from prior exposure or other unknown means," I say.

I remember the Devastation and its terrifying aftermath. We have sacrificed so much for the sake of Tajss itself. These Invaders would make all that loss meaningless. I give honor to Ladon. He must not be forgotten.

"How can you possibly believe I'm your soul mate, or whatever?" Anna asks.

She's struggling to keep moving, so I motion for a stop. I offer her my waterskin, and she gulps it down before offering it to Amara.

"I didn't believe it either," Amara says, after drinking her fill. "And no, I don't understand it, but I know Shidan and I are meant for each other. We belong together. He makes me a better person."

"But that's love, nothing to do with fate or souls," Anna says, shaking her head. "You get to know each other, you fall in love because you have lots in common."

"Maybe," Amara says.

"How do two people who have so much in common come to exist if it is not done intentionally? By fate, or some higher power?"

"How can you believe this? I was never supposed to be here! None of us were. We should still be on the ship and never even know you exist. Random chance happened, crashing us here."

I almost speak too soon. It was not random chance. The Eye predicted the human's generation ship crashing onto Tajss. That is not something I can share. Not even most of the Order know this.

"Perhaps," I say. "Or it was the hand of fate, bringing you to me, where you are meant to be."

In time, in private, I will confide in her. She is not ready for this knowledge, nor are those who travel with us. They are not Order, they do not know that we follow the visions of the Eye, who has predicted everything.

Anna shakes her head and Amara laughs, a sharp, barking sound.

"You're impossible," Anna says.

Sverre has a smile on his face, and when I glance at him, he shakes his head and motions with his hands that he's not going to be of any help. I know, in time, she will come to understand. There is no doubt she is my mate. The one chosen for me before either of us was born. The one I'm meant to love and care for.

How she doesn't see this makes no sense, but there is little I can do about it. The only worry I have now is protecting her long enough for her to realize the truth. I am hers and she is mine. We continue our travels, each of us retreating to our private thoughts as we focus on the journey.

The suns are low on the horizon. Shadows stretch across the sands and still we run. None of us have talked about Ladon or the missing Tribe. The losses are becoming too numerous to count.

Something happened on the Southern Continent sometime back when all communication was cut. Now the compound is destroyed, and only a handful of us remain. There are other outposts far away, but I have to assume that they fare no better.

Ladon wanted to attack the ship in the sky. The bunker that he uncovered holds many secrets, some even I, with all my knowledge, can only guess. There are weapons there that could aid us in turning the tide. Getting to them, understanding them, and activating them—each is a monumental task. Possibly impossible.

The City is under siege. They wait for us to weaken, but I suspect that they also wait for reinforcements. Equipment better suited to deal with the shield that protects the City.

It is full dark when we reach the door to the tunnels. Sverre opens it, and Shidan drops down first. Once he signals an all clear, Amara goes down, followed by Anna. I go and then Sverre. The journey through the tunnels takes place under a blanket of heavy silence. All of us know what comes next, and none of us want to face it.

Calista awaits.

ANNA

"No," Calista says.

She's waiting at the door to the tunnel, arms crossed, cheeks stained with tears. Our small group looks one to another, but none of us speak. I expect Amara to step forward, she knows Calista better than I do, but she hangs her head and doesn't move.

"No," Calista says, shaking her head violently from side to side. "No, Damn it, no."

"Calista," I say, but I've got nothing.

Amara walks forward, arms in front of her, but Calista backs away. My chest constricts so tight I can't breathe.

"No!" she screams, her voice trembling. "No. I told him. I told you all. No. No. No."

Her voice cracks, and the dam she's been holding back breaks. She drops to her knees, crying. Amara kneels and wraps her arms around her. Tears stream down my face too feeling her loss. I can't look. It's too painful, too personal. I'm an intruder in the worst moment of her life.

When I look away, my eyes light on Khabri. My heart

thumps hard, and something shifts, as if the world locked into a new position.

What would it be like? Could I?

I can't deny I've grown to like him. It started that he didn't scare me, but that's not all of it, at least not anymore.

I wipe the tears from my face and force a breath into my constricted lungs. It hurts. Calista is sobbing, still on her knees in Amara's arms, and the sound of her grief is a siren's call. A call that speaks not only of loss, but of love, deep and true.

It tears at my heart and soul. Ripping through my emotional shielding. I'm left defenseless before a raging storm of my own grief and loss. My knees quiver and my back spasms. I gasp, covering my face with my hands.

Images of all that I've lost parade behind my eyes. My friends, my home, people I didn't have time to get to know before any such chance was lost. The mining settlement burning. The siege of the City. The empty caves and home of the Tribe. The Zmaj whose names I don't even know, sacrificing themselves to save us humans.

Humans who hated them. Humans who don't deserve such consideration, yet the Zmaj did so without hesitation. I'm choked up, barely able to get air past the lump in my throat. Calista's grief has subsided to low sobs, but the pain in my chest pulses with a stabbing knife that is driving into my head.

I move to Khabri and place my hand on his chest. His eyes widen and his nostrils flare. I stare into his beautiful eyes. They're deep pools of azure, shining bright with sharp intelligence, but deep in them is a fire. A fire I want to warm myself by.

"I'm sorry," I whisper.

"Sorry?" he asks.

His heart is thumping hard in his chest, beating out a strangely staccato rhythm as if each beat is echoed.

"The loss of your men," I say. "Klauth and all the others."

His eyes glisten and I feel his pain. His scales are cool under my fingers. The staccato rhythm speeds up. His lips part as a tremor races through him, rustling his wings.

"They died honorably," he says.

"They died to save us," I say.

Calista's sobbing and Amara's soft words of comfort set a soundtrack to this moment, somehow serving to strengthen the connection between the two of us.

"Yes," he says. The word is breathy, almost dropping into a growl. Heat flutters in my belly. "We would all die to save you. It is our honor."

My knees quake. I could melt in his arms. It's the hottest thing anyone has ever said to me, and it cuts through the grief, the loss, and drives home into my heart. He means it. There is no hint of doubt or reservation. He would do anything for me.

For me.

My shields are down. Grief and loss and more emotions than I can name rage through me, but his words slice through all of that. Cutting deep, straight into my soul. I cling to them, the knowledge they give, and it lifts me up.

"I…" words won't form.

My thoughts are too nebulous, almost too big to squeeze into the constraints of simple sounds. My heart races as my mouth goes dry. I try to speak, to say what I mean, but it won't come out.

I throw my arms around him and squeeze tight. His massive, bulging biceps close around me, and I'm safe. Safe inside the island of his arms.

"What about the Tribe?" Calista asks.

Reluctantly, I step out of Khabri's arms and turn to face the rest of the group.

"Gone," Sverre says.

159

"Gone?" Calista asks, rubbing her face with her hands, leaving her cheeks flushed.

"It was as if they walked away," Shidan says.

Calista frowns as her face hardens, and then she says, "We need to get to Rosalind."

No one offers any argument. Calista leads the way. Her back and shoulders are squared and her head held high. Her moment of grief and weakness is left behind, here in this dry, dusty tunnel. Admiration burns in my chest. Could I be so strong if I lost the love of my life? What if Khabri died?

I'm not his fated mate. No matter what he thinks or says, I don't believe in fate. We all make our own choices, choose our own paths. No matter that though, I do see a glimmer of a path forward with him.

A girl could do worse. A lot worse. He's strong, kind, and would obviously put my wants and desires above all. That sounds nice, but is that what I want? Would he be like a slave to my will?

That would get boring, fast.

I think about the other girls who've chosen Zmaj mates. None of them seem bored. They seem… happy. The depth of Calista's grief clearly isn't the grief of a woman with a superficial love. I turn the possibilities over as we make our way through the tunnels and out onto the city streets.

The eyes of the people of the city follow us as we pass them by. Silent, begging, hungry, and devoid of hope. The ache in my chest deepens. They look to us for some sign of salvation. We have nothing to offer, and it tears at my heart.

When we walk into Rosalind's office, her stress is clearly written on her face. She's haggard, her eyes look bruised, and there are lines forming at their corners. She looks from one of us to the next and presses her eyes shut. Her lips move for a second or two. She bows her head a moment then looks and there is steel in her tired eyes.

"Ladon?" she asks, deducing the situation from his absence.

"I told you," Calista hisses. "I told all of you."

Rosalind's jaw tightens, but she nods, silent. Calista raises her balled fists in front of herself, shaking. Amara places an arm around her shoulders, pulling her closer. Calista opens her mouth, but she's shaking too hard to speak. She shakes her head and turns into Amara's embrace.

"I am sorry," Rosalind says softly.

"Sorry doesn't bring him back!" Calista snaps, breaking from Amara's embrace to confront Rosalind. "I told him and I told you I had a bad feeling. This was going to be bad, but no one listened!"

"Calista, we had no choice," Rosalind says.

A side door opens and Visidion strides into the room. He stops just past the door looking at the scene before him.

"What has happened?" he asks.

"We lost Ladon," Khabri says.

"The Tribe?" Visidion asks.

"There were no signs of them," Khabri answers.

"Bodies?" Visidion asks.

"None," Khabri says.

Visidion's head nods up and down in slow motion. His face is blank but emotions play out in his eyes. He moves across the room to stand at Rosalind's side, placing one hand on her shoulder.

Calista can't maintain her glare any longer. As tears stream down her face, she turns her back on Rosalind.

"I'm done," she says. "We're screwed."

She walks towards the door and none of us move to stop her. Her words ring too true, too painful.

"Calista," Rosalind says.

She doesn't yell but the command in her voice is intense. Calista stops, hand on the door. She doesn't turn around but she looks over her shoulder.

"What?" she asks.

"I'm not giving up," Rosalind says. "And Ladon wouldn't want us to."

"Ladon wanted me to leave with him," Calista says. "He knew this was coming. None of us listened to him. I didn't, either. If I had…"

She chokes off unable to finish her sentence. My heart is breaking for her, and at the same time I feel like I'm an intruder. What right do I have to be here? I'm an outsider. I followed Gershom, because I was an idiot, but that alone diminishes my right to be in this room.

I want to hug her. I want to take her pain away, but there is nothing I can do. I'm helpless, and there is nothing in the world I hate more than feeling helpless. The palms of my hands itch. How do I help?

Rosalind rises to her feet. She leans on her desk, bowing her head. Her shoulders slump, and I can only imagine the weight she is carrying on them. When she looks up the despair in her eyes is gone, replaced by hard steel.

"We have two choices," she says. Everyone in the room gives her our full attention. "We give up, or we fight."

She locks eyes with each of us, one at a time. When she meets my eyes, my heart leaps into my throat and adrenaline pumps through my veins. My skin tingles and the hair on my arms rises.

"I'm not giving up. Ladon's sacrifice will not go unanswered," Rosalind says. "The City looks to us for leadership. To us. We have one chance, one opportunity, win or lose. It's on us."

"What would you have us do?" Sverre asks.

"It's time we take the fight to them," Rosalind says. "We can wait no longer."

"How? We're outnumbered! You going to send the rest of our men out to be slaughtered?" Calista asks as she about faces and marches across the room to stand in front of Rosalind's desk.

"No," Rosalind says calmly. "I said fight, not commit suicide."

"How?" Shidan asks. "We are outnumbered twenty to one or more. The human males cannot stand against one Invader, much less those odds."

Rosalind sits in her chair, leaning back. She steeples her fingers in front of her face and frowns.

"Ladon thought there were weapons we could use in the bunker he found," she says. "I agree there will be, too."

"That is a long way to travel considering all the exits to the City are amass with enemies," Sverre says.

"It is," Rosalind agrees. "But we know those aren't the only ways out of the City, don't we?"

"I think it's clear that the Invaders are not here for any other purpose than the complete and utter destruction of all we've built," Visidion says. "My father has spoken to me that this day would come. That outsiders would come again to threaten Tajss."

"But why?" I ask. "Why now? Why the all-out assault?"

"They want epis," Visidion says.

"I get that," I snap. "So why don't they take it? The entire planet, as far as I know, is wide-open for the taking. Why bother with us? They can take all they want and what difference are we going to make to them?"

Visidion and Rosalind exchange a look.

"When we were off world," Visidion says. "The rumor of life on Tajss was enough to ignite a fire. We did all we could to quell the rumor, but it would seem that our allies out there have failed to contain it."

I shake my head. "That doesn't explain what's happening."

"Before the Devastation, Tajss had become little more than a glorified slave planet," Khabri says. "The Twelve Galactic Federation planets vied for control of it for epis. It was a cold war for ages until it was ignited at last. The one who started the war was from Krik. If I'm not mistaken, that is the planet that you and Visidion were taken to?"

"It was," Rosalind agrees.

"And?" I ask, shaking my head. Nothing is making any sense.

Everyone in the room seems to know something I don't. Something that makes all of this make sense to them, leaving me lost.

"Krik was known as a gladiatorial planet," Khabri continues, "even before the Devastation. A planet of primal pleasures and baser pursuits. They won't just kill us, we will be enslaved. Some will go to their arenas for the pleasure of the crowds. The rest will be forced to mine epis until they die in the work itself."

"You've got to be kidding me," I say.

"I do not jest," Khabri says.

"Gladiators?" I ask, unable to process the thoughts fast enough.

Earth history was a required subject on the generation ship, including vids of old documentaries and movies on the various eras. I was familiar with the rise and fall of Rome, but I had always thought it was more of a story, not something that really happened.

"I've been there. It's real," Rosalind says, as if reading my mind.

Calista is shaking, with grief or anger I don't know. Fresh tears well and fall down her face as she steps towards Rosalind.

"Do you have a plan?" she asks through gritted teeth.

"Yes, we have one," Rosalind says. "It's dangerous and fool-hardy. It's also our only chance."

"Tell me," Calista says. "Show me how we make the loss of my love not in vain."

Rosalind's face twists into a grim smile.

"His loss will not go unanswered," she says, unrolling a map on her desk. "Here is the plan."

18

ANNA

I CAN'T BELIEVE WE'RE EVEN THINKING ABOUT THIS. ROSALIND'S plan is insane.

Khabri walks beside me as we leave her office building. Neither of us have spoken since walking out of the meeting. My head is spinning, too many thoughts, too much information, and too much loss.

I'm a leaf in a storm, being blown from moment to moment and unable to control my own fate. Is this the hand of fate that Khabri goes on about? Am I fighting against some universal power trying to guide me to… what?

His side? Love and babies and eternal happiness? What happiness can there be? We're under siege by a far superior force, and our one hope is a two-pronged suicide mission?

"You are very quiet," Khabri says.

His voice is soft, subdued. Does this weigh as heavily on him as it does me? I eye him out of the side of my vision. He's so big, like a rock. Imperturbable is a good word to describe him, but does it mean he doesn't feel? Doesn't care? Do Zmaj feel loss and fear like humans do?

I don't know the answer. I turn my thoughts over and around, thinking about Zmaj. They're so... alien. Yet he's been nothing but kind and protective. More protective than any man I've known my entire life. More caring. Even gentle.

How weird is that? Gentle. Him. All seven feet, overly muscled, bare-chested, wings, tail and even freaking horns, and still I find him gentle.

Well, not if he's facing down an enemy. If he were like that towards me, I'd be terrified, but he's not. Not with any human. Even those who've frankly acted like jerks and probably deserved it.

Gentle.

And now I realize he's watching me with expectation, because I've been busily stewing in my own thoughts and ignoring his question. My cheeks warm as I clear my throat.

"Uh, sorry," I say, shaking my head. "I guess I'm lost in my thoughts."

"I would dearly love to know them," he says.

I snort. "I want to know yours."

He stops and I do too. I turn towards him, and he has this curious look on his face that is tinged with amazement.

"You do?" he asks.

My cheeks hurt, my smile is so big, and tears well in my eyes. Why am I being so emotional? A lump forms in my throat and I can't speak, so I nod. I reach out and take his hands, squeezing them, and nodding even more vigorously.

"I am afraid," he says.

The bluntness and honesty in his words drive into my heart. Blossoming in pain and love.

"Me, too," I say, choking on the words. Swallowing hard, I cough and clear my throat the best I'm able. "Of dying?"

He shakes his head. "No."

"Then what?" I ask.

"Of failing to protect you," he says.

My heart explodes as emotion too strong for my body swells. Trembling, I step closer. My breasts touch his chest as I reach up and cup his face in my hands. Words won't suffice. Facing certain death, and still, his only thought is for me.

And I can't quit thinking about him. About what might have been if things were different.

I tighten my hands on his face and pull down. He acquiesces, bending in, until our lips meet. Of course Khabri is far from my first kiss. Still, this is unlike any kiss that's come before it. Those weren't kisses, they were but the pressings of flesh.

This. This is a kiss. A kiss that ignites fire in my blood. It rages through my soul. His lips touch mine, and I transcend to something beyond. I throw my arms around his neck, giving myself to him.

Our kiss is tinged with desperation, not only of need, but of our situation. The kiss is a promise, not only of future pleasures, but of a future at all. We stand on the brink of imminent demise, and here we are, kissing. Yet it's the right thing.

His kiss opens the locks on my heart, and as it does, my mind opens as well. I don't know about fate, but I do know that these feelings are real.

I love him.

It's not enough to know. It's not enough to kiss. His tongue tastes my lips, which I part to welcome him home.

Home. Inside of me. Melding together to be one.

It feels right. Natural.

This is what I've been looking for my entire life, and I never knew it. He gives of himself so deeply. Holding nothing back. I've never experienced anything close to this.

When at last we break apart, I'm left with racing heart and gasping breath. Shaken to my core. We stare, silent, into one another's eyes. His cock is rock hard, digging into my belly, but he waits.

For me.

I don't think any human man would ever exhibit such control. Such submission to my will, and the fact that he does makes me burn hotter.

He wants nothing more in this world than to be mine. For me to be his, to love and protect. To keep forever.

I want nothing more either. All the reasons I shouldn't are gone.

"We should… go somewhere," I say.

"Where?" he asks.

I look around, unfamiliar with the City. It's different than when I lived here. They've made it nicer overall. It's mostly empty. The majority of people have gone to the tunnels underneath the City for what protection they offer.

Across the way is an empty building. I nod my heads towards it, grab his hand, and walk. He doesn't ask questions, and I suddenly feel powerful. He is mine. My will, his. It erases the deep, irrational fear I've always had of the Zmaj.

My warrior. My protector.

I hold the door open for him, then follow. Inside it's dark and cooler. As soon as the door closes, I grab his arm and pull him close. Wrapping my arms around his neck, I kiss him and force my tongue past his lips.

I hook a leg behind his to press my body closer to him. Our tongues move together, tasting and testing. My sense of control is heady.

I break the kiss and step back. His chest heaves, but he doesn't move. His eyes drink me, and I'm falling more in love. The way he looks at me is worshipping. I need to exercise my control. Quell the last tinges of fear.

"Let me see it," I order.

His head tilts to one side and his brow furrows. "See it?"

169

"Your cock," I say. "I've heard about them, and now I want to see it."

He smiles, and then undoes the tie of his pants, letting them drop to the floor. My eyes widen and I gasp. It's everything every rumor said and more. My god!

His cock is rock hard, straight in front of him with a slight curve up. It looks as big around as my wrist but more than that, there are ridges down the top. The ridges slope back towards his groin. I follow them down and see there is a protrusion of bone at the base.

"Wow," I say.

"I am glad you are pleased," he says.

"Can you... stroke it?" I ask.

My mouth is dry, my heart racing, and my pussy is so wet I feel it on my thighs.

He doesn't speak, grabbing his cock instead and slowly stroking. Impossibly, it grows larger. I grab my tits through my shirt, rubbing the rough fabric against my nipples. This is stupid. Under siege, and he's going on a suicide mission.

Which is why I must do this. Control. I need the control.

His eyes are heavy, half-closed but focused only on me. Slowly I undo my blouse and expose my tits to him. The speed of his stroking increases and his tongue darts out, licking his lips.

My breasts are full, not large, but a handful as I take each of them in my hand and lift, rub them for his pleasure. His groan is all the answer I need. I trace the nipples with my fingers, making them harder, more erect.

He steps towards me, but I stop him with a look.

"Not yet," I say, my voice throaty.

Butterflies and fire dance in my stomach. Watching his muscles ripple as he strokes his cock before me is incredibly sexy. He doesn't move except for his one hand working that huge cock, gripping it tight and stroking faster.

"Slow," I command, and immediately he slows his motion.

I smile, warmth flushing my skin.

Moving deliberately slowly, I undo the fastening of my pants. They part in a Y, revealing the first hints of my womanhood. His eyes dart from my tits to the small exposure of my pussy, and once more, his strokes speed up.

I want to watch him blow. I want him to spill his seed in tribute to his love for me. I want to create a future with him that I don't even know if we'll have.

Fear, doubts, and outright terror edge every feeling with desperation.

"Faster," I whisper, pushing my pants down over my hips.

My pants drop to my knees as he strokes his dick faster for me. I wriggle my legs to force the pants down further then bow my legs outwards to expose myself.

I run my hand over the soft hair and press down on my mound. The pressure on my clit makes me shiver. I can't take my eyes off his hand stroking his cock. It's hot and sexy. He wants me. He's mine.

I slide two fingers inside my wet and ready pussy, curling them up, seeking that magical spot that will drive me crazy.

He groans, his body wavering, then he takes a step closer. His hand moves faster until he's jackhammering his cock with rapid strokes up and down its considerable length.

He leans towards me, but I can't take my eyes off his cock. I finger myself in time to his motion. An orgasm is building so fast that I can't slow it down. My knees quake. I put my hand on his chest, the rock-hard muscles exciting to touch.

We stroke faster and faster, working our bodies in time to each other.

I'm moaning, and he groans. He falls towards me, catching

himself with his free arm on the wall behind me. I lean back against it. The material is cool against my back, offsetting the fire of my skin.

His cock is aimed at my belly. He strokes faster. Faster.

I rub myself, driving slick fingers in and out.

His cum hits my stomach like a bullet. It splashes across me in long, sticky streams. At the same time, I fall over the edge into a full orgasm. My body is wracked by the power of it.

Muscles clenching tight, spasming.

"Oh god," I cry out, holding fingers deep inside myself.

His cum keeps spurting out. Loads and loads of it, blasting against my belly, dripping off, dropping to the floor. I lean my head against him, letting the last of my pleasure pass.

He hooks an arm around my shoulders, holding me up while the aftershocks of my orgasm pass. His scales are welcoming and cool against my forehead.

When the last of the quakes pass, I look up into his eyes and we kiss.

The desperation gone, this kiss is slower. Deeper. More intimate still than what we have just shared.

As we kiss, his hands move up and down my back. I straighten and lean into his touch, pressing my body against his.

His cock is hard again. I pull back and look down, amazed he could be ready to go again so fast.

"Wow," I say.

He lifts my chin with two fingers, tilting my head back, and lays claim to my lips. He hooks his arm under my ass and lifts.

I wrap my legs around his waist. His cock rises to press against my slick entrance. We don't break the kiss. He lowers me.

His cock pierces me, and I gasp in surprise and pleasure. I'm so wet it slides in easily, but I've never felt anything like this before.

I slide down his shaft until he's fully seated inside. Our kiss burns hotter, passion's aroused, and I grind my hips against him. Running my hands through his hair, I catch his horns, and acting on a whim, I pull his head back, kissing my way across his cheek and down his neck.

"Yessss," he moans.

I close my eyes, throw my head back, and circle my hips.

"Fuck," I moan.

He feels so good. As I suspected, that protruding nub at the base of his shaft hits my clit perfectly. I'm filled to bursting, and that pressure against my pleasure button is driving me towards a fresh orgasm.

I bite my lip and lift myself up, down, swirl myself against the nub, then repeat the motions.

Khabri holds me up effortlessly. He moves his hips perfectly in time, sensing my intention until we're moving as one person.

He grunts with each thrust. It's the hottest damn sound, so primal, full of his need and desire. When I open my eyes, his are wide, studying my face with so much devotion it makes me shiver.

His horns are spiraled with small ridges that I hadn't noticed until I felt them. I stroke both the horns while using my legs and hips to keep up the pleasure motion.

"Ugh," he grunts thrusting harder.

"Yes," I encourage. "Faster."

He shifts his weight and then leans over. I'm almost parallel to the floor while he holds us upright with his one hand on the wall. Now he goes for it.

His hips jerk back, and then he drives himself home, burying his cock fully inside me in a single thrust. I gasp, eyes widening, my entire body tingling and flaming at the same time. Before I can take my next breath, he pulls back and does it again.

"Huh, huh, huh, huh," I exclaim with each thrust.

I close my eyes, riding the wave. Pleasure builds to a resounding crescendo, and I jerk myself tight against him as the waves of it crash together. Through the resounding finish, I feel his man juice filling me up, and a niggling thought occurs that we haven't used any protection.

And, no matter all I've said, it's okay.

His seed filling me represents hope. Hope of tomorrows yet to be. Risings of the suns that we might witness together. Of things we might do to make a better world for our children.

As the final waves pass leaving me limp in his arms, I cling to him with what little strength I have left. He straightens, his cock softening inside, and then slowly pulls me off of his dick. I lower my feet to the ground, unable to stop the ridiculous grin on my face.

He cups my face in his hands, kissing me with a soft intensity that speaks to needs and desires as-of-yet unfulfilled.

"You are my treasure," he whispers.

"I…" I trail off. I what? I'd almost said I love you. Almost, but then rationality crashed in, and the words wouldn't come out.

I want to. I do. I think. He's smiling, waiting. I need to say something, anything at this point because now I feel like a damn fool.

"I know," I say, running my hands over his face, trying to show him how much more I mean.

He places his hand flat on my sticky belly, staring at my stomach with adoration.

"Our babies will be mighty leaders," he says.

I push his hand away, shaking my head.

"You're impossible," I say, grabbing my clothes.

19

KHABRI

It is difficult to focus. She is exotic, distracting, and so beautiful it aches.

Our joining was more than I had ever imagined. Now it preys on my thoughts. I can't stop watching her move. I don't want to.

After we've dressed, she places her hand on my chest and then rests her face against me. I wrap my arms around her and hold her. Neither of us break the silence, knowing the next words we speak will propel us back to reality.

The siege, the war, the impending destruction of all we've known and loved. Yet, I know it will work out. Somehow. I cannot believe that Tajss would bring us together at last, only to have us ripped apart.

I will face doom, but I will do so with hope. I have known the love of my one true mate. She is the missing piece of my soul and now, at long last, we are complete. The only thing that would make this moment any more perfect would be to know for sure that young life grows inside her, but it is much too soon to know this.

The ground rumbles, breaking into our quiet moment, calling us to action.

"Are you sure about this?" she asks.

"We will succeed," I say.

"You sound awfully certain," she says.

"I am," I say.

"How? How can you be? There are thousands of them. They outgun and outman us!"

A smile stretches my mouth so wide my jaw hurts, but I can't stop it.

"Because I have you," I say.

"What am I going to do to stop all that?" she asks, waving her arm towards the dome.

"You are the fuel of my heart, the essence of my dreams, the very air that I breathe," I say. "Having finally found you, I will extinguish the fires of the stars to assure your safety. They will not stop me."

Tears fill her eyes, she bites her lip, and then shakes her head.

"That is the corniest thing anyone has ever said to me," she says. "And the loveliest."

She rises onto her toes and kisses me. Her soft, unscaled arms wrap around my neck as we keep kissing. Lips tasting, tongues teasing, not letting the moment go an instant sooner than we must, but the press of duty does not let us stay for long.

We break our kiss, holding onto each other still. I stare into her eyes, and I know her desire to stay here. Safe, in my arms, and I feel the same. Would that we could, but my dragon rumbles. She must escape, and we don't know how long we have.

"We must go," I whisper.

"I know," she says, but neither of us move to break our embrace.

She presses her forehead against mine. The silence between us is comfortable but compressed. Outside our small bubble of safety, time races like sands across the dunes. We are stealing this moment from its grasp, but time wants it back.

She feels it, too. Slowly she releases her embrace, her fingers lingering against my neck as she steps back. My hearts slow as I close my eyes and apply my years of training. Finding my own center and immersing myself more fully into the moment I am in. Pulling all my attention away from the past, the future, until I am completely focused.

In this condition, I am hyper-aware of every bit of sensory input. The scent of dust and mold in the air that mixes with hints of our spent passion. The temperature of the air, the way light refracts and plays off of her skin. The brightness of her soft, tentative smile.

Everything is clear and known. I miss nothing. Including a soft, low vibration that in any other state I would never be aware of. Something is amiss.

I take her hand and guide her along with me out the door of the building. A shadow falls across the street as if clouds pass between us and the suns. But it is no cloud.

A ship. One so massive it blocks the suns as it moves into position over the City.

"Oh," Anna gasps, her grip tightening on my hand.

I remember ships like this. Planet breakers. It carries weapons of such destructive force that the shield over the city will not hold. A dim cheer echoes to us from outside the dome. The Invaders celebrating the arrival of what they've been waiting for.

"It's time," I say, staring at the monstrosity moving over our heads. "We must act now."

"We're not ready," she says.

"We don't have a choice," I say.

177

We run, heading for the tunnels and the launch point of our plan. No matter my words of certainty to her, and I do believe them, there is always the chance. Fate isn't static. No matter that Tajss intends us to be together, it doesn't mean we will make it.

It's up to us to create our future together. Tajss only sets us on our paths, guides us, and intends for us to make it.

She isn't ready for this knowledge, and I will not have her scared. Giving her what hope I can was the right decision. She doesn't yet accept her fate. I'm not going to fool myself. The humans do not see mating as we Zmaj do.

Zmaj mate only with their one true mate. The other half of themselves. Desire doesn't come upon us for others, but I've pored every file on the humans. Studied every scrap of knowledge the Order had to offer, which was considerable, and I know it is not the same for them.

I will not have her dawning understanding shaken with nuances of the truth. When she is ready to understand, she will. For now, my duty is to keep us both alive, no matter the odds. Besides, I believe we'll survive. We beat the Invaders before, and we can do so again.

"Khabri," Anna says, breathing heavily. She doesn't slow, though, she keeps pace with me. "Are you... sure about this?"

"I am," I lie.

My dragon recoils. Lies are not honorable, but the truth serves no purpose but to scare her. We reach the building that leads to the tunnels. Most of the Zmaj are gathered here. Through the open door that leads down to the basement and the tunnels comes the sounds of the humans.

"About time," Shidan snaps.

My men from the Order compound come to attention, and as one they glare at Shidan, tightening their grips on their lochabers.

"You saw?" Sverre asks.

"I did," I say, ignoring Shidan. "We are out of time."

"I agree," Visidion's deep voice comes from behind my shoulder.

Everyone in the room turns to see that he and Rosalind have entered the room. Anna moves closer, sliding her arm around my waist. She is the only human in this room besides Rosalind herself.

"Now is the time I would give a rousing speech," Rosalind says. "But I have no words to share. We all know the odds. We have one shot, and to say it is a long one would be an insult to your intelligence."

The other males chuckle and we all stamp the butts of our lochabers on the ground creating a resounding echo in response to her words.

"Warriors," Visidion says. "We will protect our mates and all of the humans. Are you ready?"

We roar our agreement. I squeeze Anna against my side and raise my fist into the air. When I glance down I see fear and admiration writ across her face.

As the roaring subsides, Anna lets me go. Slowly she steps backwards, moving towards the door to the tunnels. Tears shimmer in the corners of her eyes. She raises one hand to her sweet, full lips, pressing her fingers to the soft flesh. She purses her lips then motions, moving her hand towards me and blowing softly across it.

My hearts are so full it hurts. I motion catching the kiss she blew to me and then press it against my chest, pushing it into my heart where she will always loom largest. She turns and walks through the door.

As the rest of the warriors and I funnel out of the building and into the street, Rosalind says her goodbyes to Visidion before she follows Anna. They exchange a kiss. The love between them is so obvious, it makes my own pain ache worse. I look over my shoulder to the door that Anna went through.

I will see you again, my treasure, I vow.

"Sir," Titus says, stepping up beside me. His twin, Typhon is on my opposite side.

"Any advice?" Typhon asks.

"Fight with all you have," I say. "Fight for the future."

The twins nod, and as one the males of the Order stomp the butts of their lochabers. The sound echoes off the walls.

We file out of the building. The ship overhead has blocked out the suns. The city is cast in shadow, as is the outcome of our attempt. The males of the Order form in a tight square formation, the other four Zmaj huddle in a group of their own. Visidion walks to me.

"Are your warriors prepared?" he asks.

"We are," I say. "If we hold a tight form, we'll be able to withstand the onslaught the longer."

"I agree. A box shape, three males to a side," Visidion says.

"You were a warrior before?" I ask, impressed with his strategic thinking.

"I have become what I must," he says.

There's nothing more to be said. We march towards the dome. The critical part we play in our plan is about to start. No one talks until we arrive at the edge of the city. Staring at the glimmering dome and its waning protection.

The Invaders have moved back, which is good. They've retreated to the top of the closest dunes. Close enough to the dome that we can't walk out and away, but far enough that they won't be in the direct line of the blast from the ship hovering overhead.

"This is it!" Visidion yells. "Protect your treasures!"

The bijass surges through my thoughts, stronger than I've felt it in what seems a lifetime. Red tinges my vision as my fists clench tight, desperate to close on enemy flesh. It's a struggle to resist and if it is hitting me hard, then I can only imagine how it is affecting the rest of the males who do not have my years of training.

Titus throws his arms wide, chest thrust out, and bellows a challenging roar. It's infectious. The rest of the males follow his lead. Our roars rise to the heavens, and I know in my heart that Tajss hears us. Now if only it's within her power to deliver us to the other side of this challenge.

We're answered with a loud whining and the shadows lightening. Above, the bottom of the massive ship is opening to reveal a bright red-blue light. they're preparing to deploy their weapon, and we're not ready. The humans will not have had their chance to reach safety yet.

We must act now or lose before we try.

"Now!" I yell.

Visidion punches a code into the airlock. There's a crackle then a pop sound. The temperature leaps higher as the shield drops. We charge the Invaders, who look on in disarray.

The timer in my head starts. Every second we purchase with our blood and sweat matters. The humans will need all of them we can buy if they are to reach safety.

The Invaders rouse and charge to meet us.

20

ANNA

BLAM!

Dirt falls from the ceiling as we're all thrown from one side to another. Screams so high-pitched they hurt fill the tight tunnel.

"Faster!" Rosalind's commanding voice cuts through the din easily.

Everyone does. The mothers gather up their children into their arms. Illadon runs beside Calista, pulling her forward with him in front of me.

"Come on, Mommy," he yells.

Has she told him? Does he know what happened to his father? I don't know, and now isn't the time to find out. It only turns my thoughts to Khabri. What if he doesn't come back?

Is there even a what if? All the Zmaj are on a suicide mission. No one is labeling it that, but it is. A dozen Zmaj warriors against what looks like thousands of Invaders? What chance do they stand?

Our one hope at survival is to follow these tunnels out beyond the City and hope that they've caused enough of a distraction to allow us to slip past. If not… I'm not going to think about if not.

BLAM! BOOM!

Another bomb drops. It's too soon. They shouldn't be bombing yet. The entire plan hinged on getting the Invaders close enough so that they wouldn't use their ship to bomb us. Does that mean they've already fallen?

Tears run down my face, mixing with the sweat and dirt. The ground rumbles, louder and louder, not stopping now. The tunnel fills with dust, making it hard to breathe.

There had to be a better way. He's going to die. They're all going to die. It's not right or fair. I could love him. Now I'll never know.

"We're almost there, keep running," Rosalind yells.

"See Mommy, we're doing good, keep running!" Illadon says.

My heart breaks looking at him. He's a small man, well not all that small. He's past Calista's waist in height and already he looks muscular. He dresses like the rest of the Zmaj men, only wearing a loose pair of pants, cinched at his waist. His chest is muscled and his stomach flat and tight. He's not fully grown into his body yet, obviously, but looking at him I see the man he's going to become.

The mix of human and Zmaj shows so clearly on his face, more than anywhere else. His horns are small nubs, at least right now. But his face is Calista's. Round, wide set eyes, a high fore-head, and he has her nose. His chin and jaw must be Ladon's, strong and almost sharp but the rest of him is his mother.

I could have a baby like that. It's the one thing Khabri has made clear since the moment we met. He wants babies, and he wants them with me. I'm still not sure about that, even if we survive this and end up together.

I've heard the tales. Twelve months of carrying a Zmaj baby, the last three of those on strict bedrest. Doesn't sound like a good time or something I'd want to do.

But... Illadon tugs at my heart, singing of possibilities. Futures that could be, any one of which would be better than the reality we're living in.

BOOM! CRACK!

Another explosion rocks us. More dirt falls from the ceiling but that crack sets my nerves on edge, jerking all my attention back from the daydreams. I step to the sidewall of the tunnel to let the people pass. Studying the ceiling, it's hard to see through the dust, but I need to see the structural integrity of the tunnel.

There. One of the thick beams that defines the structure has a long seam running the length of it. It's not going to hold for another round of bombing. I look down the tunnel and my heart races. There are too many people still. We need to move faster.

"Rosalind!" I yell, fighting my way through the crowds.

I pass by Calista and Illadon and Illadon glares but I don't have time. I call for Rosalind again and she looks over her shoulder frowning. When I wave to show her I'm the one calling her name, she steps to the wall.

"We have to get them out of here," I say. "Now."

"We're moving them," she says.

"If another explosion hits near us, this section will collapse," I say.

"What?" "Here?" "Now?"

Panic rises among those close enough to hear. It's infectious, spreading like a virulent disease. The fear of the herd swamps rationality. People push against each other, trying to force the persons in front of them to move faster.

In moments, the crowd becomes a mob. Shouting, screaming, pushing, and pulling. It's a flat-out riot in an enclosed tunnel only big enough for four humans abreast. Horror washes over my senses as I realize what I've done.

I did this.

Screams split my ears, stomping feet, and everyone fights to move but little progress is made. The crowd surges, and I'm smashed against the wall. I can't draw a full breath—a mass of bodies makes it impossible.

Horror edges towards terror as understanding comes of how bad this is going to be. Rosalind's disapproving frown makes it worse. I want to meld into the wall and hide. She exudes an aura of being austere, almost cold, but in control. Her sharply intelligent eyes look over the panicked crowds. Her pursed lips part and she inhales as she draws herself up to her full height.

"ENOUGH!" she yells.

Her voice is a slicing blade. It pierces through the panic, cuts the confusion, and drives into each person. Almost instantly, everyone stops, their heads turning to her.

"We are better than this," she says.

She doesn't yell but the pitch of her voice reaches easily up and down the tunnel. A low murmur hums through the crowd, and then people are helping the fallen and they're moving. They become a flowing river, moving faster than they did before, but in harmony. Each person helping another person, no one pushing or crowding.

"How did you do that?" I ask, shaking my head to make sure I'm not dreaming.

"Experience," she says. "Don't do that again."

I drop my eyes to the ground, and my cheeks burn. "I'm sorry."

"Fine. Now tell me what you see."

"The support beam is cracked. One more bomb, and this section at least will cave in," I say, pointing up to the beam in question.

"Then we need to move," Rosalind says.

"Everyone, we need to move faster," Rosalind calls out. "Help each other, get us out of this tunnel. Follow me!"

She pushes her way to the front and people let her pass without her saying another word. Her presence alone creates room as she moves. I follow in her wake.

When she arrives at the front, Amara is there with Malcolm on her hip. Malcolm smiles as we arrive.

"It's going to be okay," he says.

I smile, but the butterflies in my stomach and adrenaline making me feel like my skin is buzzing tells a different story. He's being reassuring, which is cute, but doesn't calm me down in the least.

My heart is pounding, and we're all but running, but still, it's not fast enough. The back of my neck tingles, and the hair on my arms is standing on end. Imminent danger so close it's a pressure pushing against me, making it hard to breathe, hard to even think.

Something touches my arm and I look down. Malcolm's small hand rests on my forearm. His hand has tiny scales which dance with an almost iridescent color ending with sharp black claws instead of nails for his fingers.

"I know," he says, when I look up to his face. "It will be okay."

"Thank you," I say, unsure what else to say.

Amara is haggard too. Her hair is a mess, her eyes sunken, but she forces a smile when our eyes meet.

"Trust me, he knows things," she says, huffing as she shifts him from one hip to the other.

"I can walk Mommy," Malcolm says.

"Not yet," Amara says.

Malcolm doesn't argue, staring ahead with dreamy eyes. The crowd stops moving, we've come to the end of the tunnel. Rosalind climbs the ladder and works the latch on the trap door.

She opens it and sand drizzles past her as she peeks out. A moment later she pushes it up and over, then climbs the rest of the way out.

One by one, people climb methodically out of the tunnel. There are so many humans down here this is going to take forever. Time crawls past, accented by creaks and groans from the structure of the tunnel.

I stay, pressed against the wall, watching and studying the tunnel. I know what I'm looking for, but if I see it, I don't know what I could do about it. I'm feeling so much pressure that I can barely breathe. Sweat rolls down my back until finally the last people arrive and begin the climb. I help them up before following myself.

The rungs of the ladder are hot to the touch. Almost to burning. As I climb, one hand over the next, I realize the real reason I've stayed down here until the end. Safety and my 'expertise' are an excuse.

I don't want to see.

That's the truth. The real reason is, I don't want to see what's happened to the Zmaj. To Khabri.

We all know their mission was suicide. They were putting themselves out as a distraction. A desperate attempt to buy us time to escape and the vain hope we'll reach the bunker, and from there destroy the Invaders.

But they'll be gone. Dead.

I don't deserve this from them. None of us do. How can one person's life be worth more than another's?

Gershom and all his stupid rhetoric about humans first. First over what? What makes us better than any other race? Sure I never really believed his shit, but I was scared of them, and I followed him. Like an idiot.

Halfway up the ladder, I stop. Bowing my head, eyes closed, I vow to never let myself act out of fear again. All it did was lead me down a path of blindness and stupidity. Something inside myself resonates as I accept that I've been a fool, but knowing that I can be better.

I can't change the past, but I can my future. My future with Khabri.

If I have one. My arms tremble as I try to force myself up the rest of the ladder. I know I must, but I don't want to. If I don't go up, he's alive.

Sweat pours into my eyes as my heart races. I'm breathing too fast and my head is spinning. I can't do this. I can't face it. I don't want to know.

"Anna, come on," a female voice says.

I tell my eyes to open and look up, but nothing happens. Damn it, I can't stay frozen here. This is stupid.

"Anna? Are you okay?"

"I'm… I'm fine," I say.

I force my eyes open and reach for the next rung of the ladder. One rung. He's fine. Next rung. He has to be fine.

I emerge from the tunnel onto the oppressively hot sands. People grab and pull, helping me out the rest of the way. We're milling around in a massive group but I turn back towards the city. I'm numb. The protective armor clanking into place to protect me because now that I'm up here, I have to know.

Rosalind is a few feet away, lying flat on the dune. I crouch and make my way up to her side, lying flat. Calista, Amara, and Jolie are all here. I force myself to look. I can't look, but I must look. Blinking rapidly, I turn my head. My neck cracks in resistance.

The Zmaj stand in a square formation, protecting one another's flanks and backs. There are piles of dead Invaders surrounding their formation, but it's not enough. They're completely surrounded. Every Invader they kill is replaced by two more.

Even more Invaders surge beyond the ones they're fighting. The ship hovering over the city, so big its shadow reaches almost to where we are, has a glowing bright light beneath it. I barely have attention to spare for that though.

Where is he? Cold chills chase along my limbs, leaving goosepimples in its wake. I don't see him, but he has to be okay. Wouldn't I... feel it, or something? Isn't that what all this fated mate bullshit is about? I'll somehow know if he's hurt?

I knew it was a load of crap. I don't feel like he's gone or hurt or anything. All I fear is scared. Terrified that I'm losing a good thing before I even have it. How can I lose so much so fast when I've barely tasted it?

No one on the dune says a word. I'm sure each of us is looking for our mates.

Mates. Wow I have fallen, haven't I? But it's true, and I know it. He is my mate. The one I want to be with. The one who makes me feel.... Whole.

Is this what he really means when he talks about fate? Is this what real love feels like? This empty ache in my heart because he's out there, in danger? This fear that I'm about to lose him?

"I see him!" I exclaim, rising up.

Rosalind grabs my shoulder and pulls me back flat.

"Stay down," she hisses.

My cheeks flush at her admonishment, but my heart is racing and butterflies dancing in my stomach take more of my attention than the embarrassment. He's right there. I don't know how I missed him.

He's fighting next to two of the guys who are from the Order like him. They're amazing. They fight as if they're one person. Their lochabers weaving in and around each other in an intricate pattern that any weaver would be proud to create. With every pass of their blades, blood flies from an enemy.

If only it was enough.

The Invaders surge forward, those behind the front line shoving in. The front line falls to the whirling blades of our guys, but the surge pushes them back, into each other. Now their blades don't fly as fast. They're tangling with each other.

The surge doesn't stop. Fresh Invaders climb over the bodies of their fallen, rabid, insane in their willingness to throw themselves at certain death. Except it's no longer so certain.

One of the Zmaj falls. I can't tell who it is, but the other men close the gap left, moving so it looks like he's inside the protection of their box.

The Invaders press in and two more Zmaj fall, including one next to Khabri. My heart is in my throat. My head pounds in time with its beating. Waves of nausea pass over leaving cool sweat in their wake.

I want to look away but I can't. We're the sole witnesses to their sacrifice.

"We have to go, now," Rosalind orders, belly crawling backwards from the edge of the dune.

"No," I say, shaking my head.

"I won't have those men die in vain, it's on us," Rosalind hisses. "Now move it."

Reluctant I crawl backwards. My last sight before the dune cuts off sight is another surge by the Invaders. I'm half-way down the hill when it happens.

AHOOOHA – AHOOOHGHA – AHOOO

Everyone stops and the sound comes again. Scrambling at the sand which suddenly decides to turn loose and slippery I fight to reach the top of the dune again.

As soon as I reach the crest, I see it.

Past our fighting men, beyond the hordes of Invaders, cresting another dune stands a huge man. There is a massive thing that looks like it's made from a bivo horn in his hands. He raises it once more to his lips and the resounding sound echoes across the sands to us.

"LADON!" I exclaim, jumping to my feet like an idiot.

Hope swells my chest and races along my limbs. I realize I'm being stupid too so I drop to my stomach but stay where I can see. The Invaders halt their assault looking up at the lone man blowing a horn.

What in the hell is he doing?

Then I get it. More figures join him along the crest of the dune.

"The Tribe!" Jolie exclaims.

21

LADON

I BLOW THE HORN ONE LAST TIME BEFORE DROPPING IT ON THE sands.

"Are you ready?" I ask Drosdan at my side.

"I was born ready," Drosdan growls.

I raise my lochaber high into the air. The sun glints off the blade, and the rest of the Tribe members raise their weapons to match.

"Now!" I yell.

We charge with a resounding roar. Racing across the sands, ready to deliver our wrath on the Invaders. My left wing is broken, making it harder to stay on top of the sand, but adrenaline fills my veins, burying the pain.

The Invaders far outnumber us, but this isn't a final battle, it's a rescue. We're here for the people in the City. Why the males are outside fighting isn't clear yet, but there are no doubts about the ship in the sky. The City is going to fall.

We slam against the Invaders, and the chaos of battle forms. Drosdan is a mighty warrior, and I'm glad he's by my side, not that I'll ever tell him why. I'm too slow. My blade doesn't move as quick as it should. My reaction time is a whisper off, but that whisper is too much.

When I made the tunnel collapse, I was resigned to my own death. Lying under the rubble and sand, barely able to breathe, the pressure increasing with each breath, I knew my life was over.

Except I couldn't let it end.

Calista and Illadon were in my thoughts, as they always are, but if I let myself die there, they'd be without protection. In danger.

Rage stoked in my core, burning away the touch of death herself. I struggled and fought. Fought for each breath. Fought to find a way free. I fought until I had nothing left and still I was trapped. Unable to escape no matter how hard I tried, but I couldn't have it end like that.

I did the only thing I could. I prayed.

I prayed to Tajss. The mother of us all . . . and she answered. I'd never been a male who subscribed to such beliefs. The Order, in my thoughts, were fanatics giving themselves over to some unknowable future.

I was never that way but now....

Now everything has changed. Tajss heard my prayers. Calista is mine. My mate, my treasure, and my time with her is not done. As I lay crushed and desperate, the ground rumbled. I was sure that more collapse was coming.

The rocks crushing me shifted and breathing came easier. With breath came hope, and with hope, fight. I fought to free myself as the ground continued to rumble and the debris to shift. It took what felt like the passing of ages, but at last I crawled free of my tomb and came face to face with a zemlja.

It lay on the sand, mouth open to reveal its row after row of teeth. It lay there, but it didn't move. Didn't raise itself to fight or threaten. I thought, for a moment, it must be dead, but I could see the movement of its breath. Smell the rot of debris in its exhale.

I rose, shakily, to my feet, staring at the creature. As I stood on knees weak from exertion, a guster walked around the zemlja but it did not attack either. Its cold dead eyes stared, watching with the cold calculation of a hunter.

A loud screech split the air, then a sismis dropped from the sky to land on top of the zemlja. Its wide wings rested across the worm's breadth.

I stood staring at the three apex predators. One from below Tajss, one that walked Tajss, and one that ruled Tajss' skies.

I stared and I knew. Tajss herself sent them, they were my rescue. Their message clear. My duty is not only to my family, but to her. These Invaders must be driven off of her.

Strength filled my crushed, broken, and abused body. I lowered myself onto one knee, bowing my head. The sismis screeched, the zemlja rumbled, and the guster growled. Earth, air, and sky gave me life but it is not for my sake.

We fight for all life on Tajss.

Another Invader falls before my blade to reveal Sverre.

"Well met!" Sverre yells, ducking under an Invader's swinging blade.

The Invader follows the blade up with his club, which catches Sverre in the side. I yell a wordless sound as I strike down the Invader.

"Where are the humans?" I ask.

"Escaping," Sverre says, his brow furrowed in pain but he continues to fight. "We're buying time."

Understanding comes as to why they are out here fighting.

"It's time for us to leave," I say.

As if in time with my statement there's a whoosh followed by a rumble. The instant it happens, the Invaders look up with fear on their faces, then turn and run. The dimness caused by the shadow from the ship overhead lightens, and I look up.

The bottom of the ship glows brighter than it was. So bright it hurts my eyes, and my protective lenses snap shut to filter it. The bright light coalesces with bolts of lightning, then it forms a blue-white beam that slams against the dome over the City.

"Run!" I yell but everyone already is.

I'm heading north but suddenly I shift direction to the west. It's not thought, but a feeling, a knowing that this is what I need to do. On top of a far dune is a flash of white. Blinking rapidly, I squint, and a moment later see that it's Rosalind.

Standing next to her is my treasure.

My hearts explode with love, desire, and the protective rage of my dragon. My treasure, but not my son. I wave my arms wildly, trying to order them to run across the distance.

Dim memories of seeing these before, during the war that created the Devastation emerge from the fog of the bijass. My stomach clenches and the dragon rumbles. A planet breaker ship hangs over the City. It won't be long before it breaks through the shield. Once that happens anyone in the blast radius will be evaporated.

"RUN!" I bellow.

The Zmaj are, for the most part, well-trained warriors. Samil looks around with confusion on his face, but a moment later he's moving too. The warriors of the City and Order shifting reveal the fallen they were protecting.

I grab Sverre under one arm as Shidan grabs him from the other side. He's conscious but severely wounded and unable to run so we drag him between us.

The very air crackles as the weapon of mass destruction powers closer to its peak. Once it is fully charged, it will unleash devastation.

"FASTER!"

We're too slow. My hearts thump harshly, thrumming against my chest. The growing ionization of the air is making my scales tingle and itch. As I inhale the tingling affects my lungs, making every breath strangely unpleasant. As if my lungs are being frozen and electrified at the same time. There's a metallic taste on my tongue that grows stronger.

We crest the first dune, where Calista and Rosalind were but they either understood my message or figured it out on their own. I see them two dunes ahead of us. Good but not good enough. We're all still too close.

"We're not going to make it," Shidan says.

"I know," I say, shaking my head.

"Keep running," I say. "Only chance."

He nods as both of us lower our heads, leaning into our run.

"Leave me," Sverre says.

He kicks his legs trying to get himself to his feet. My bijass surges, clouding my thoughts, that primal instinct to protect what is mine, to dominate, agrees with Sverre. He is not my concern, another male is a threat, not an ally. My duty is to Calista and Illadon.

It surges, spewing its base instincts, but breaks against the indomitable rock of my own will. I am a warrior and we do not leave our fallen brethren behind.

"Don't be a fool," I growl.

He struggles until he is on his feet. Blood drips from multiple wounds but he lurches along so I let him run on his own.

He stumbles before we reach the top of the dune but Shidan and I catch him. He steadies himself without stopping.

"They're not far enough," Shidan says.

He's right but there's nothing I can do. The humans run in a mass herd. There are too many of them for me to pick out

Calista but I do spot Rosalind. Her white armor stands in stark relief against the sea of dark colors the rest of them dress in.

She is at the rear, herding her people. A true leader, she doesn't go to safety herself until her people are.

The ground rumbles and then buckles. We're thrown forward. Instinctively I spread my wings and white-hot pain explodes through my body, blinding me. I hit the ground. My head cracks against something, and blood runs into my eyes.

I'm tumbling head over heels coming to a halt on my back staring up at the red skies of Tajss. I roll onto my side, every muscle in my body crying out in protest. There is nothing that doesn't hurt, but as I fight through the pain, I hear Calista's voice echoing through my thoughts.

Ladon. Help us. We need you.

"I come, my love," I cry out, pushing past the pain and the failures of my body. "Tajss grant me strength, I come."

On my feet again, I'm stumbling alongside Sverre. Shidan rejoins us as we fight our way forward. The ground itself is jumping. Every step forward takes an incredible amount of effort.

We lean onto each other, resting our arms across one another's shoulders to give what support we can. The ground bounces so hard my teeth rattle in my head. Sand dances, rising up, crashing down.

We fight for every bit of forward motion. Another dune. Almost to the top.

"Daddy!" Illadon yells.

I see my mate and son as we reach the top. Illadon yells, but he's pointing behind me.

Turning to see what my son is looking at, I see the blinding white-blue light, pushing dirt and sand like a wall racing down on us.

22

KHABRI

I'M THROWN BY THE BLAST. SAND, DIRT, AND ROCK TEAR AT MY scales as I tumble through the air. Holding my wings closed, I curl into a ball and ride the wave, preparing for the impact I know will come.

As I tumble, all I can think of is Anna. Her soft face, the taste of her lips, the way her skin feels under my fingers. Even the sound of her voice, which is music in my ears. She is my sun and stars. She is all, and somehow I must live, for her.

Did she escape? Hope is a sputtering, flickering flame that I must keep alive. I hit the ground and blackness consumes thought.

Pain.

White flashes behind my closed eyes. Struggling to pull my thoughts to coherency. I open my eyes and see... nothing.

Everything is dark. The air is filled with dirt and sand. It's hard to breathe.

"ANNA!" I yell, choking on the air. I strain to hear her, to hear anything. Nothing.

Hands held in front of myself, I move. My foot goes down, too far, and I fall again. The pain gives me focus. I feel around with my hands. The ground is destroyed. Rough to the touch, where before it had been smooth sand, now it's ragged. I touch something hard and cold.

I run my fingers up and down it. It's long and twisted. It takes a moment to realize the material is metal, most likely a part of a building's structure.

"ANNA!"

I climb out of the trench and resume my search.

"CALISTA!" Ladon's voice reaches my ears, so I make my way towards him.

I bump blindly into him.

"Who?" he asks.

"Khabri," I answer.

"Calista!" he screams, his voice breaking.

"Anna!"

We walk shoulder to shoulder, keeping touch as sight is useless.

"HERE!" another voice calls out.

"Sverre?" Ladon asks as we grope our way towards the voice.

"Yes, my leg," he says.

The filth in the air swirls, but when we're close to Sverre and I crouch low, it's clearer than when I'm standing. Clear enough to see Sverre.

He's struggling against a large, twisted iron beam that rests on his legs. He strains to lift it but the thing barely moves.

"Ladon, grab there," I point to him and again to the far side.

Ladon does as directed and together we lift. My body protests, but I push through and lift with my legs. The metal screeches as it finally gives way, rising high enough that Sverre is able to pull himself free.

His legs are a mess. One of them lies at an odd angle, clearly broken, the other looks shredded. Dried blood covers it with blackness. Kneeling next to him I grab his head and force him to look at me.

"Find your center," I say. "Go deep, where you go when the bijass surges and tries to assume control."

He nods understanding, closing his eyes. I keep my grip on his head and wait. Shidan stumbles up to us hurt as well but Ladon deals with him.

"Okay," Sverre says at last.

"Good," I say. "Now, think about all that you live for. Think of your futures. Of your child and children to come."

He nods and when he opens his eyes calm falls across his face. "Can you brace the leg?"

"Yes," I say.

I crawl around on my hands and knees until I find parts that will be serviceable. A length of metal and in a jagged crevasse I find remnants of wiring.

"Ladon, Shidan, hold his arms," I order. "This will hurt."

Sverre nods his understanding as the two males take his arms. I run my hands down his broken leg, feeling the lay of the bones. Once I can visualize them as they are in my head I take a firm grip. I jerk down and left, pulling the bones into place.

Sverre bites off his cry of pain. I use the material I found to fashion a brace for his leg that will hold the bones more or less in place. It's the best I can do for now.

Ladon and Shidan help him up. They each have one of his arms over their shoulders to keep him upright. We don't need words to resume our search. Our mates are all that matters.

"The City is—was there," Ladon says, shifting his tense mid-sentence, and pointing behind us. "The humans should be this way."

He leads us across the broken ground. We have to alter directions more than once to work our way past chunks of building material that wasn't incinerated in the blast. I can't see above us so I don't know if the ship is still up there or not.

A weapon such as they used on the city takes time to charge, so if they are we have time before they'll be able to fire it again. Time that we must not waste.

"ANNA!" I yell again.

"Here!" her voice is distant and off to our right.

I run towards it. Desperate to hold her in my arms. The other males struggle to keep up, having to help Sverre.

"Ladon?" Calista voice comes to us.

They sound distant but the filth in the air makes it impossible to judge distance. I slow and help the other males to keep up. It's against every urge I have but I am not an animal or a primal barbarian. I am a warrior and a male. I will keep my honor.

"Anna! Keep calling, we're coming!"

"Here! Here! Here!" her voice is cut off by coughing.

I wave my free arm in front of myself hoping to make contact with her. When I touch flesh I grab on and pull it closer.

"Hey," Calista says when we're close enough to see each other.

"I apologize," I say, guiding her over to Ladon.

"Khabri!" Anna cries out, throwing herself around me.

Her lips pressing to mine. Explosions fire through every cell of my body as I wrap my arms around her. She wraps her legs around my waist, her arms around my neck, and we give ourselves to each other.

The other females find their mates but that is happening distantly. Beyond what matters. She is in my arms. She is alive.

I knew it but feared it otherwise still. She is my mate. My treasure. She is all that I will ever need, and if I lose her I would not be able to go on.

"I thought I'd lost you," she says, gasping air when she breaks our kiss.

"Never," I say. "I am yours."

Tears stream down her face drawing lines through the dirt on her cheeks.

"I'm yours," she sobs. "I love you."

My dragon bellows, and I can't hold it within myself. Throwing my head back, I roar. No words, raw emotion, ripping out of my heart and challenging the universe if it would dare to take her from my arms.

"I love you!" I follow up my bellow. "My treasure! Mine!"

"Yes," she sobs, kissing me repeatedly. "Yes. Yes. Yes. Yes. Yes."

She accents each yes with a kiss on my lips.

"We need to move," Rosalind's voice cuts into the reunions.

The dust cloud is clearing, slowly still, but the sky and those close to hand are visible. The Zmaj males of the City are reunited with their mates. Calista and Ladon stand hand in hand, their child on Ladon's hip. Ladon and I lock eyes and he nods.

"Yes," I agree with Rosalind.

Ships whiz over our heads. Fresh troops will be landing and we are in no condition to fight. The humans didn't make it to the bunker but we must make it there now.

"Brethren!" I yell to be heard and the males of the Order snap to attention, no matter their injuries. "Help the humans. This isn't over. We must reach the bunker."

No one questions my commands. I look at Rosalind who is barking more orders. I'm sure we lost some people but we have one chance at survival. We make the bunker, or we die out here on the sands.

We set to our tasks.

"There," Amara says pointing. "That will get us inside."

The doors to the military bunker open for her and we herd our mob of survivors inside.

Anna stays at my side and I never want her to go from it again. We assist the humans inside while the Zmaj form lines to either side to give aid as needed. Once the flow of people is going, I climb the nearest dune so I can survey what we left behind. Anna walks with me, her arm around my waist.

"They killed their own people," she says.

"No, not their people," I say. "The Invaders, as you call them, aren't 'their' people. Those are clones, created for one purpose. To die."

"That's horrible," she says. "They're still people."

"Perhaps," I say. "But not so in the eyes of those behind this invasion. Their masters, if you will, care only about controlling the epis. That's why we have to stop them."

"How can anyone be so callous?" she asks.

"I don't know," I say.

She shields her eyes from the suns as we study the wreckage. The city is gone. A dark silhouette of shadows is all that remains. A handful of building infrastructure that looks like the bones of a giant reaching for the sky. Even from here I can see that the metal frames are bent and twisted by the force of the blast.

Those are only in the center of what was the city. Past them, which looks like six or seven blocks, is a crater. It scars the surface of Tajss where the blast rolled out on its path of destruction. The dome is destroyed and effectively every building too. The debris of their remains litters all the way to the horizon.

"Oh," Anna gasps.

The massive ship still hangs in the sky over the crater. Doors open on its sides and troop ships pour out. They haven't even dented their forces.

"We need to get inside," I say, turning back to the bunker.

When we get back to the door most everyone has entered the bunker so Anna and I do the same. I've never been in here before but I heard rumors of it. Even before the Devastation it was a story to scare people. Terrifying experiments done on living subjects.

I didn't believe it, until I joined the Order. Only then did the truth of my people become known, at least some of it. There is no time for exploration now, we need to figure out any weapons there are to hand and how to use them.

"This way," Amara and Shidan say in unison.

I follow them while the other Zmaj and their mates follow suit.

"Everyone else," Rosalind says, her voice echoing off the walls. "Stay together and work to create a temporary home. Set up kitchens, sleeping quarters, and everything we'll need to survive in here for a while."

The crowd murmurs and whispers. It's loud in this enclosed space but no one argues with her or the points she makes. Slow, almost reluctantly, they set to work while the rest of us follow Amara.

She leads the way through the bunker with ease until we're in a massive room. Yellow rails surround a huge hole in the ground.

"That's it," Amara says.

A bank of dead computers, covered in dust, line one wall. I walk over to the railing and look down into the darkness. I can barely see what looks like a metallic sheen down there. Lights come on then flicker fitfully, not helping to see deeper into the hole but I have a good idea what is in there.

The missiles Ladon wants to fire. I study the ceiling and it does appear to have a seam, so I think he is right.

"Anyone know how to operate this control board?" Rosalind asks.

The males of the Order have gathered close around my position. I look over my surviving members.

"Vae," I order. "Attend the computers."

Vae nods as he rushes over. His hands fly deftly over the crystal controls. In moments they've come to life and he is studying the read outs. Rosalind and the Zmaj of the City and Tribe look at me but I watch Vae, ignoring them.

"They're all staring," Anna whispers.

"They are," I agree.

"Doesn't that bother you?"

"No," I say. "They were not ready for this knowledge."

"Oh," she says, but something in her voice pulls my attention to her.

"What is it?" I ask.

"Is there things you aren't telling me because you don't think I'm ready?"

"Or there hasn't been time," I say.

"Not an answer," she says. "Look, if we're going to be together, I don't want to have to wonder. I want to know you. Know what you know. I want us to be working together, not hiding things from each other. That's a deal breaker, got it?"

I smile. "I do."

"Quit smiling like that," she says. "You look like a cat with a mouse."

"What is a… 'cat'?" I ask.

She rolls her eyes. "Forget it."

"Sir," Vae says.

"Report," I say.

"The Invaders are surrounding our location," he says. "And the ship… is moving towards us as well."

Cold and silence greets his words. My stomach tightens and a chill races down my limbs.

"Options?" I ask.

"I can get the missiles online," he says. "I think."

"Thinking isn't called for here," I snap. "Yes or no?"

"Yes sir!" he exclaims, snapping to attention.

"Do so," I say. "Now."

He whirls around and sets to work. Rosalind and Visidion approach. Rosalind's brow is furrowed, and she looks angry.

"You not only knew about this bunker, but your guys know how to fire the weapons?" she asks.

"As you can see, not exactly," I say.

Her eyes narrow. "Do not play word games with me."

I meet her stare. She's much shorter than I am but she has a presence that fills the space around her, making her an equal, no matter the height difference between us.

"Of course," I acquiesce. "We didn't have hard data on this, no, but we did have some tech still, which Vae is skilled in operating. He should be able to extrapolate from what he knows to make this work. Or so I hope."

"So say we all," she mutters. "So say we all."

A loud thump echoes off the walls seeming to come from all around us. It's followed by another and another in fast succession. It's as if some giant child is banging the sides of a box, using the bunker as a makeshift drum.

A human rushes into the command room, eyes wide with sweat pouring down his face. He looks around wide-eyed until spotting Rosalind, and then he runs toward her.

"Rosalind," he huffs. "They're attacking the doors."

"Shit," Rosalind curses, looking at Visidion, then me. "We need to put warriors on the doors. If they break through before we end this, we're in trouble."

"Agreed," I say.

"I agree, my love," Visidion says.

"Order!" I call out and all my males come to attention.

"Tribe!" Visidion barks and his males do the same.

"You know our duty," Visidion says. "Our mates, our families are in danger. We must protect the doors while these others attempt to bring weapons on-line."

The males nod understanding and then slam the hafts of their lochabers on the ground. The sound echoes and ends with a sudden, final silence.

"Well? What are you waiting for? Go!" I say.

They run for the front doors, leaving only the leaders in the command room.

"Vae, report," I say.

"Almost there," he says. "I think I'll make it."

As if in response, there is a loud screech of metal on metal and then sunlight streams in through a crack in the ceiling. As the ceiling parts open, an amber force field springs to life around the pit.

"There are only two missiles," Vae says.

"Then don't miss," I say.

Anna squeezes my waist tighter. She fits against me perfectly. Her head rests on my chest and her arm rests perfectly around my hips. As if she was designed exactly for the space. My treasure, my mate, the love of my existence.

Smoke rises inside the force field, then a rumble so deep I feel it in my bones. I step back, pulling Anna along with me. Even as we do, a shadow falls across the opening in the ceiling.

"The ship is almost in position," Visidion says.

"It's also unloading a lot of warriors," Rosalind says. "My god, how many do they have?"

"There is no shortage," I say. Anna trembles in my arm.

"Sir?" Vae asks.

"What is it?" I ask.

"It's ready," Vae says.

"Fire," I order.

There is an intense roar as flames pillar up and press against the force field. The temperature in the room rises and then the missile comes into view, fighting gravity. It's as if it moves in slow motion, clawing its way up with destructive intent.

Cold assails my chest and limbs. I turn my back on the monstrosity and wrap my arms fully around Anna. Doubts and fears tear through my thoughts. Resting my chin on her head I close my eyes and lean into my training to control myself.

This is everything I've fought against as a member of the Order. A weapon of destruction so vast it defies all I know to be true. The rumble shakes me to my bones as it rises. I hold my treasure tight, praying to Tajss that this is the right thing.

23

CALISTA

"No, you don't get to run off again," I say, grabbing Ladon's arm and jerking until he turns to face me.

"Cal, my love," he says, stopping, and I don't miss the wince of pain when I pull. "Now isn't the time."

"Now is the *only* time!" I yell. "I thought I lost you!"

He grimaces, and his scales tinge with shame and regret. He bends down and his lips meet mine, his arms embracing me, and almost I forgive him. Almost. Breaking the kiss, I pull back.

"No," I shake my head. "You left. You… you… died!" Damn it, the tears won't stop. "I thought I'd lost you."

"I know," he whispers. "I am sorry."

"You're sorry?" I snap angrily. "Not good enough. Do you have any idea what I was going through? How was I supposed to tell Illadon that you weren't coming home? I told you not to go. I knew something bad was going to happen. How did you survive? They said you were buried."

"I was," he says.

"How?" I ask.

He frowns and shakes his head. He opens his mouth to speak, then stops and snaps it shut. At last he inhales deeply, then pulls me out of the hall we're standing in and into a side room. It's a small room with banks of monitors lining the walls.

The sound of the Invaders beating on the doors to the bunker echo down the halls, but I don't care. I need to understand this. The others can hold them at bay without Ladon. My stomach is still a tight ball.

He looks around as if making sure we're alone, then guides me over to a seat. He takes a seat in front of me, head bowed, and studies the floor for a long time before he meets my eyes.

"Tajss saved me," he says.

"Tajss?" I ask.

"Yes," he says.

I wait for him to say more, to explain himself, but he doesn't speak. He seems to be studying the backs of his hands where they rest on my thighs.

"And?" I ask, prodding him to continue.

"I don't… know how to explain it," he says, raising his gaze to mine. "I was buried, trapped, barely able to breathe. All I could think of was you and Illadon. How much I love you and how I couldn't be there any longer…."

He's a blur through the tears, barely an outline. Cold chills form pimples on my arms and even my breath feels as if I'm in a freezer. The emptiness I felt when they walked out of the tunnel and he wasn't with them is back, even though he's here with me now.

"Ladon…" I choke. "I can't… not without… I'm…"

His fingers touch my cheeks, tracing the line of my jaw. He grabs my head and tilts my face up to him then kisses each cheek, drying my tears before he claims my lips.

He's here. He's safe. We're safe. I'm not alone.

"Calista, Tajss saved me, for you," he says. There's a tone to his voice I've never heard before, a sound of reverence.

"That's crazy," I say.

"It is," he agrees. "I know, but Cal... my treasure..."

He trails off. I wipe my eyes clear so I can see him. His beautiful, strong face is covered in filth as we all are. There are small cuts marring his scales, and trails of blood mix in the dirt, drawing strange patterns.

I throw my arms around his neck and cling to him. I can't let him go. There's a fear, deep in myself, that this is an illusion. I've cracked, fallen off the edge, and he's nothing but an illusion. He feels real. Solid. Mine.

"I asked you not to go, why did you leave?"

"Cal, I tried to take you and Illadon away," he says. "I didn't understand it, but I knew we had to get away. I know a place we could have made ourselves a home, away from all of this."

"We couldn't leave them all behind," I say.

"I know, my treasure. Your heart is large, you embrace everyone."

A smile tugs at my face, but I push it down because I'm still angry with him.

"You shouldn't have left," I say. "I told you I had a bad feeling. If we're all going to act on our inspirations, you should have listened to me. I almost lost you!"

"Yes, my love," he says. "I'm sorry. I wanted to take you to safety, but if I couldn't do that, I had to do whatever it took to protect you."

"Ladon," I murmur in his ear. "I love you. I love you so much. I can't do this without you."

"You could," he says. "You are the strongest of females."

"Not strong enough," I whisper. "Not for another child without you."

He tightens his grip, pulling me against him. The two of us cling to one another, then he pulls his head back.

"What?" he asks, my words sinking in.

I smile, but the tears are streaming again. I can't hold them back. It's the hormones. It must be.

"Yeah," I laugh and cry as I shake my head. "Yeah."

"You're… do you mean?"

I can't get words out, so I shake my head smiling, no matter that I'm scared.

"By Tajss!" he bellows, leaping to his feet, carrying me along with him and spinning us in a circle.

"Hey," I cry out. "Easy, easy, easy." Thankfully, he stops spinning me around. "Still in the morning sickness stage."

"I am sorry, Cal," he says, peppering my face with kisses. "I am so…. happy. How long have you known?"

"A while," I say.

"Before I left?"

"Yes," I say, cheeks warming.

"Why didn't you tell me?"

"I didn't want to use it to make you stay," I say.

"I do not understand."

"Ladon," I say, cupping his face in my hands. "I love you, but if you stay or go, I want you to do so on your own decision. Not because I manipulated you to do it."

"Cal, that makes no sense," he says. "You are my soul mate, how could you manipulate me? That would be as if I were manipulating myself. We are two halves of the same. I know this more than ever. Tajss has revealed truth, the symmetry of life is irresolute."

"You really have had a spiritual awakening, haven't you?"

He nods slowly. "Yes, my love, I have. I see it now, so clearly."

The floor rumbles, vibrating me to my core. We look around at the monitors, now flickering to life. My stomach falls to the floor seeing them.

"Is that… outside?" I ask.

Thousands of Invaders cover every inch of sand. Machines blast the doors we came through. Ships zip through the sky, unloading still more Invaders and above it all hovers the massive ship that blasted the city, moving slowly into position.

"It is," he says. "but it will be okay."

"It will be okay?" I ask shaking. "There are too many of them. And that ship!"

Ladon smiles and shakes his head.

"Tajss did not save me to die like this," he says.

"I'm glad you've found faith, but Ladon, seriously, what are we going to do?"

The rumbling increases, louder and louder, drowning out all other sound. The monitors flash with a bright light. There's a loud boom, and darkness engulfs us.

24

ANNA

THE EXPLOSION OF THE MISSILE THROWS KHABRI AND ME against each other. He wraps his tail around my waist as his wings snap open and flap to keep us upright. The lights in the room go out as it happens. My ears are ringing, and I bit my tongue.

"Report!" Khabri yells, not letting me go.

"One moment," Vae responds.

He curses as the rumbling of the floor stops and we're no longer fighting to stay upright. Turning in his arms, I look blindly around the dark room, then up through the opening in the ceiling. Fire roils across the opening, massive boiling clouds of flame. An instant later, debris bounces off the opening, and I flinch.

"It worked!" Vae exclaims excitedly.

The few people left in the room cheer, and I do too, but looking at the fire through that opening makes my stomach clench tight. The sheer destructive force is terrifying. Unbelievable. All those souls outside must be dead. And how many people were on that ship?

The lights come back on in the room. Khabri releases his

tight grip letting me stand on my own. I stay by his side as he walks over to the controls. Rosalind and Visidion stand beside us and together we watch the monitor.

At first, it's nothing but the cloud of fire, but that burns itself out and then we can see the empty sky above the bunker. Vae moves his hands over the crystals on the desk and the view changes. Black marks and some metal debris mar the otherwise normal sands of Tajss all around the bunker.

"Sir?" Vae asks, looking at Khabri.

"Rosalind, shall we implement Ladon's plan?" Khabri asks.

"Make it so," Rosalind says.

Khabri nods and Vae goes to work. It isn't long before the now-expected rumbling begins.

"This is the last missile," Vae says.

"Good," Rosalind says. "I don't ever want to see such destruction again."

We turn and watch the missile blast into the sky. This time it goes out of sight, and there is no explosion to watch. Turning to the monitors, we can see it arcing through the sky. Vae watches a screen with symbols and numbers flashing across it.

Anticipation and fear tie my stomach into knots. It's a final blow that will eliminate the threat to Tajss but the destruction the first missile caused is terrifying.

"Hit," Vae says. No one speaks, waiting for him to say more until at last he turns to face Khabri. "It's gone sir."

"Good," Khabri says.

"So… it's over?" I ask.

"Yes," Khabri says.

"This battle is over," Rosalind says. "I am not going to be so fast to assume the war is over too."

"We have bought time," Visidion says. "But there can be no doubts that there are those in the galaxy willing and able to bring war to Tajss."

"True," Khabri says. "It is not for us to live in fear, though. Let us make the most of the time we have bought."

Cheers echo from the halls outside this room as the rest of the survivors hear the news that it's over.

"Khabri, you speak for the Order," Rosalind says. "I would invite you and your mate to sit in council with us."

"Thank you," Khabri says. "I will."

I bite my lip looking at Rosalind. I can't not speak up. I try to keep the words inside but they won't stay.

"Rosalind, you know… who I am?"

"Yes," Rosalind says, looking at me with her imperious stare.

"You know… what I did? You want me on your council?"

"Why would I not?" Rosalind asks.

"I followed Gershom," I blurt it out. "I was banished with him. I was stupid, sure, but… you…"

Rosalind's glare causes me to lose my train of thought and I stumble over my last words.

"Anna," Rosalind says. "Gershom was a foolish man, yet I did not, nor have I ever, wished harm on him or any of his followers. If the Zmaj and human race are to survive, we need every one of us. Even the fools."

My cheeks burns red hot, I'm not sure if that's a compliment or an insult but either way, she wants me here. She forgives me, something I didn't know I wanted but knowing it, a weight lifts from my heart. I look at Khabri and the love I have for him is set free with the lifting of that burden.

I've made mistakes. I've done stupid things, but those things are my past. They don't define me now or mean I can't do better in the future. And I am better, because of him.

"Let's take some time to celebrate," Rosalind says. "We'll meet tomorrow and begin putting together our way forward."

Visidion puts his arm around her shoulders and the two of them walk off together. Khabri and I walk out of the control room without a word, each of us knowing the other's intention without them.

As the door closes behind us, I turn into him and rise on my toes. Our lips meet in a gentle, soft kiss. I nibble his lip, tugging at it. His tongue swirls in my mouth as his hands work to free me of constricting clothing.

"Anna," he breathes my name, and I shiver as his breath brushes across my fevered skin.

"Khabri," I say.

He explores me with his lips and the lightest of touches. We work our way into a bunk room, managing not to fall in the tangle of our falling clothes. As he lowers me onto the bed he continues kissing.

The bed creaks as he places his weight. His massive body hovers over mine, his rock-hard cock brushes against my leg.

I run my fingers through his hair and grab his horns. I pull him into a deep kiss. Our tongues tasting of each other until we break to breathe.

Staring into his deep, soulful eyes, I believe. All of it. Call it fate. Call it destiny. Call it what word you will, and it doesn't do this justice.

We belong together. It's right in a way that nothing in my life has ever been before.

The bed protests as he climbs on the rest of the way and shifts his hips. I spread my legs, welcoming him inside of me.

Where he belongs.

Together.

His cock slides in, and it's like two pieces of one part coming together. This isn't sex. Sex doesn't describe this.

Our bodies join together. Our bodies are having sex, but it's unlike any sex I've ever known. I'm complete.

Full, spiritually and physically. His cock drives in to the hilt.

"Khabri!" I exclaim my pleasure as sensation rushes through me.

He's mine. I'm his. We're one.

He pulls out to the tip. He reaches down, grabbing his shaft, and then he moves it in a circle, using the head to explore my folds. When he finds my clit and rubs up and down, I can't contain a shudder as I'm overwhelmed with pleasure.

He pulls away and I groan, pulling down on his horns, wanting to be filled. He rises onto his knees, grabs my hips, and flips me over.

I rise, pressing my ass back against him, and he shifts and enters. He doesn't hold back, thrusting in deep, and we find our rhythm.

He grabs my tits, teasing the nipples with one hand, slapping my ass with the other. He brings his tail around and places it on my ass, shifting until it puts pressure on my virgin hole.

I bury my face in the pillow, not wanting to be heard, but unable to contain my voice.

Reaching between my legs I rub my clit as he pounds my pussy faster and harder. He's close and so am I. When he drives in and holds, lifting me up so that I'm impaled on his cock, the orgasm takes over.

Muscles clench, stars explode in my vision. I'm left shuddering in the aftershocks of the most forceful orgasm I've ever experienced. He spills so much seed into me that it runs down my legs as he lowers me to the bed.

He pulls out and moves around until we're lying next to each other, my head on his chest, listening to his breath.

"I love you," I whisper.

"I love you," he says. "And our children. And our life. I am filled with joy such as I've never known."

For the first time, I don't feel the recoil at the thought of kids. Actually I feel… excited? Intrigued? Desirous even?

"Have we won, for real?" I ask.

He doesn't answer at first. His fingers play with my hair, trail down my shoulders, then back.

"No," he says at last. "We have, though, bought time. Time to prepare."

"How long?" I ask.

"I don't know," he says. "We will need to make the most of it."

"What is this place?" I ask.

"A place of nightmares," he says. He shifts onto his side, resting his head on one arm.

"What do you mean?"

"The Devastation was set in motion in this place," he says. "It is a place of great evil."

"Why do we stay here then?" I ask.

"We won't, not for long," he says. "This must be a temporary respite while we find suitable arrangements to replace our homes."

"Do you have any ideas?"

"Not yet," he says. "Tajss will provide though."

I smile at his words. "Do you really believe that?"

"I do," he says, tracing my cheek with the tips of his fingers. "How can I not? It brought you to me."

"I don't know if I believe all that," I say. "But I like the idea."

"I will believe enough for both of us," he smiles.

His hand trails down my side coming to rest on my hip. He shifts again, lowering himself, until he's kissing my stomach.

"Our children will be strong," he says. "Leaders for the future. The world they will inherit is what we create for them."

"You're awfully certain of yourself," I grin.

"Tajss will provide," he whispers, kissing my belly and working his way lower.

I give myself over to his renewed pleasure. Perhaps he's right. Tajss will provide. If not Tajss, he will. Of that I am sure. As sure as I am of our love for each other, and that new life grows in my womb.

If you missed it, start at the beginning with Dragon's Baby (Red Planet Dragons of Tajss Book 1).

If you want to know more about how the survivors arrived on Tajss read the prequel Red Planet Dragons of Tajss (Red Planet Jungle).

JOIN MIRANDA'S READER LIST
USA TODAY BESTSELLING AUTHOR

SUBSCRIBE TO BE THE FIRST TO KNOW WHEN THE NEXT RED PLANET DRAGONS OF TAJSS STORY IS OUT!

SIGN UP NOW@
Tny.sh.mirandamartinlist

ALSO BY MIRANDA MARTIN

Red Planet Dragon's of Tajss Series

Red Planet Jungle Series

The Power of Twelve Series

The Alva Series

Dragon's & Phoenixes Series

ABOUT THE AUTHOR

USA Today Bestselling Author of fantasy and scifi romance, Miranda Martin's books feature larger than life heroes with out-of-this-world anatomy and smart heroines destined to save the world. As a little girl she would sneak off with her nose in a book, dreaming of magical realms. Today she brings those fantasies to life and adores every fan who chooses to live in them for a while.

She was born and raised in southern Virginia, but as a veteran she's traveled to places like Korea, Hawaii and good 'ole Texas. Now she's settled in Kansas, the heart of America, with her husband and daughters. Her favorite animals are dragons, unicorns and cats. If she's not writing, you can still find her tucked away somewhere with a warm blanket and her nose in a book.

Get in touch!
mirandamartinromance.com
miranda@mirandamartinromance.com

facebook.com/mirandamartin
twitter.com/imMirandaMartin
instagram.com/imMirandaMartin